KINGFISHER CLASSICS

THE STORY OF
ROBIN HOOD

From the first minstrel tellings,
ballads and May Games

Retold by ROBERT LEESON

Illustrated by BARBARA LOFTHOUSE

Kingfisher

For Joanna, Mia, Simon, Suzannah
and Thomas

KINGFISHER
An imprint of Larousse plc
Elsley House, 24-30 Great Titchfield Street
London W1P 7AD

First published by Kingfisher 1994
2 4 6 8 10 9 7 5 3 1

Text copyright © Robert Leeson 1994
Illustrations copyright © Barbara Lofthouse 1994

A CIP catalogue record for this book
is available from the British Library

ISBN 1 85697 254 2

Designed by Caroline Johnson
Edited by Caroline Walsh

Printed and bound in Italy

CONTENTS

LISTEN, ONE AND ALL

L isten one and all, to my tales of Robin Hood, of how he lived and what he did, who were his friends and who were his foes, why some hated and many loved him and how he met his fate at last.

Some say Robin was a forester's son. Some will tell you he fought and killed a dozen foresters when he was still a lad of fifteen. Some say his mother was high born, but loved a servant. Some say his uncle was a squire. Others will have you believe he was an earl who lost his title, his castle and his lands – and so became an outlaw.

But only this is true: Robin was born neither high nor low. He was a yeoman outlaw. But he was more. He was King of the Summer, Lord of the Greenwood and the Prince of Thieves. He had no need of castle or land when he could range ten thousand acres of forest, sharing them only with the King of England.

Why was he an outlaw? I will tell you. There are times when it is easier to be an honest man outside the law than within it.

Shoot a deer in the Royal Forest and the Sheriff's men will hang you, if they can catch you. Take your dog hunting and they'll hack off his claws – by the law. Cut a branch or a twig from the greenwood and they'll thrash you for it.

Better to live free an outlaw in the forest than live a slave at home.

So, young men came to find Robin Hood in Barnesdale on the higher ground or Sherwood on the lower. When the deer left the dales and sought the shade of the woods, Robin followed them. When the Sheriff of Nottingham pressed him too closely he drew back to the dales by ways he knew and the Sheriff did not. And where Robin went, we followed.

He hated moneylenders who sucked the blood of the poor. He was hard on wealthy churchmen who were greedy and told lies.

But Robin was no godless thief, believe me. He would never sit down to eat without prayers to his Lady, the Virgin Mary. For her sake he would never harm any woman – even when, once, a woman did harm to him. That was his way.

He would take no money from ploughman or cottager, nor from yeoman farmer or servant. Knights and squires were safe with him – if they were well-mannered and told the truth.

How was he to look at? How to tell you? Lithe, sunburnt and light on his feet. There were men who were stronger – like Little John. Some, like Gilbert of the White Hand, could match him with the longbow. Will Scathlock, or Scarlet as he was called, could beat Robin in a straight fight with sword and buckler. So why did we follow him? Because he led the way. He went where others did not dare. He was so reckless that sometimes others would cry halt. But what did he care? If he made up his mind, he would go alone, whatever the danger.

Laughter was easy for him. He would joke as soon as fight, sing as soon as shoot. But his eyes were keen. They saw right through you. Robin could read a man's face – did he lie or did he tell the truth.

And he was a master at disguise. More than once he walked the streets of Nottingham, into the Sheriff's house and out again, and no one the wiser. He fooled them all.

But in the end, Robin Hood was deceived. Only treachery could overcome Robin.

We followed him, sometimes three score, sometimes seven score, when there was gold in the strong box. When times were hard a few stayed close to him. But in the best days, the sound of his horn would bring a hundred and forty running from miles away. In summer we made lodges of green boughs under the oak tree and the lime. In autumn we went to our caves. Where? I'll not say. Some will tell you they know. They put Robin's name on any hole in the ground.

Yes, many tell tales of Robin Hood that never shot with his bow. I know and I will tell you what I know.

THE STRANGER ON THE BRIDGE

No man ever beat Robin Hood in fair fight and got away with it – for a good reason. If he ever met one who could get the better of him, Robin would persuade that man to join his company – to put on the green hood and tunic and make a new life in the forest.

In this way he found the best and won them to follow him. So Robin always gained the day, whoever lost the fight.

Will Scathlock, or Scarlet as they called him by the colour of his stockings, fought Robin half one day with sword and buckler, until the blood ran down. In the end they called a halt and Will was Robin's man ever after.

George-a-Green, the Pindar of Wakefield: he was minding the cattle one day when three young men in green came marching through the corn. He challenged them. They laughed at him. He took them on with sword and quarterstaff and battled them to a standstill, some say one by one, some say all at once. And that was worth watching, for those three rogues were Robin Hood, Will Scarlet and Little John.

Such were the men who followed Robin, and the mightiest of all was Little John. Seven feet tall from his crown to his heel and broad as a barn door; fierce in battle but calm and always ready for a joke. A good man for a friend, but a bad enemy.

Little John came along when Robin was young – maybe twenty years old and full of tricks.

One morning in the woods, near Nottingham, he told the band to wait for him while he roamed around on his own in search of entertainment. "I've had no sport for a fortnight," he said.

Off he went alone and the track took him over a stream. Only it didn't take him across this day, because the wooden bridge was only wide enough for one and there was a man on the planks already, so big he blocked the bridge from rail to rail. Robin stepped on lightly to see if the stranger would make room for him.

Instead he spoke roughly: "You stand back till I cross, lad, or I'll give you a taste of this on your back." And he wagged a great quarterstaff at Robin, who did not take that kindly at all.

Quick as light Robin unslung his bow, slipped an arrow from the quiver at his side and notched it.

"Don't talk like a fool, man," he called. "I could send this through your heart before you could even touch me."

The stranger eyed the arrow point aimed at his chest and answered scornfully:

"Spoken like a true coward. Bow against staff? What match is that?"

Robin flushed red with anger. "Coward? Not me. If that's what you think, I'll put my bow down and fight you hand to hand."

Then he got back his good humour and, whistling, ran to the bushes to cut himself an oak staff with his hunting knife. Trimming twigs and leaves, he hastened back to the bridge.

"Right, friend," he said cheerfully. "Let's give it a trial. The one who puts the other in the water is free to cross."

"Agreed!" With that the other swung his stick across his chest as Robin rushed forward, oak branch whirling. He came on so fast the big

man was taken aback and took a knock on the crown that flayed his skin and sent the blood streaming down.

"One to you," he grunted. "But I pay my debts." He switched hands so rapidly that Robin never saw the blow until it caught him across the back and drove the breath from his chest.

Then it was thrust, strike and block like farmers threshing corn, till all of a sudden Robin felt the end of the stranger's staff deep in his belly, followed by one across his head that tipped him like a sack of corn over the rail and into the swiftly-flowing brook.

As Robin struggled in the water, the giant, wiping the sweat from his red face, leaned over the rail. When he got back his breath he shouted, "Now where are you, me lad?"

Robin spluttered and laughed and yelled back, "Going downstream fast."

Wading ashore, he pulled himself out onto the bank by a low branch. Gasping for breath, he blew first a weak, wavering call on his horn. The stranger laughed. Robin blew again, more strongly. And again.

Then the big man stopped laughing as out of the bushes the men in green came running. First there was Will Stutley.

"Master! What's happened? You're like a drowned rat."

"Think nothing of it," laughed Robin, shaking his shoulders. "Ask him on the bridge. He put me in the stream."

"Did he, by the Rood?" Stutley ran forward with a half dozen outlaws and took hold of the big man. "Let's see how he fancies a ducking."

"Lay off," roared Robin. "Let him be." Then to his opponent he called. "These are my men. They'll not harm you."

The stranger looked over the crowd in Lincoln green now leaning on their bows in a circle around him.

"All your men, eh?"

"That's it. Will you join us? A man with your

talents is more than welcome. And what you don't know, we'll teach, like how to bring down the fallow deer at a hundred paces. What d'you say?"

With barely a pause, the answer came. "I say yes."

"Then tell us your name and where you come from."

"I'm from Holderness, eastwards, and sometimes I'm called Reynold Greenleaf."

"Sometimes, eh?" Robin glanced shrewdly at the speaker. "But what do they call you when you're at home? I guess that must be some while back."

"I'm called John Little."

"John Little?" Robin's men burst into laughter and Will Stutley struck John on the shoulder.

"Little. That's false for a start." To the others he added, "We'll re-name him. We'll... baptize him."

With that the whole company struck off into the woods taking secret paths until they came to the great clearing under the mighty Trysting Oak. Its branches spread so wide that a whole army might shelter under them.

Here, Robin's men formed a ring and Will Stutley took up a leather jug of strong ale. Then in a voice high and whining as a priest's he declared, "This infant is called John Little. I hereby name him Little John."

The ale was emptied over John's head and the trees shook with the chorus: "Little John! Little John!"

ALLAN-A-DALE

The sound of singing rose from the valley, coming closer, louder. The singer was in good voice. Slowly it faded away into the distance.

"There goes a happy man," Robin told Little John.

The tall man nodded. "Right. And a handsome one. He comes past each morning, early. On his own."

"What like is he?"

"Well turned out, dressed in red from top to toe – like a wedding guest."

"If that's so, why haven't you stopped him? He should have something in his purse for us. He uses our highway freely enough."

Little John shook his head. "Seemed a pity, Master, to stop a happy man."

"Ha," jeered Robin. "You'll stay poor and that's the truth. I'll take a look at this singer myself."

Next morning early, Robin waited at the head of the slope in the shelter of the trees. But this time there came no sound. Pushing through the undergrowth he looked down on the trail below. True there was no song, but there was the singer. No spring in his step, he shambled along not looking where he was going. And, worse still, he'd left off his red tunic and was dressed in dull brown.

"Hey, hey, not a wedding," thought Robin, "a funeral more like. I must know why."

He whistled sharply and in a trice Little John and Much came out of the forest and ran down the slope. As he saw them, the traveller faced about, snatched the bow from his back, notched an arrow and took aim.

"Stand off," he called as the two reached the trail and blocked his way. "What are you after?"

"Put up your bow," answered Little John calmly, "and come with us. We'll do you no harm, but our master wants a word with you."

Soon enough the young man with his escort stood under the trees facing Robin. He was wary but there was no fear in his eyes.

"Well, minstrel," Robin began, "day after day you've sung your way through our greenwood – and paid nothing for the right of passage. Now, what have you got in your purse for Robin Hood and his men?"

The young man shook his head. "Five shillings is all I have in the world."

"Let's see them."

Without hesitating the young man held out his hand. Five small silver coins glinted in the sunlight. Robin looked him in the eye. That was true, he thought. Yet he asked, "Nothing else?"

Slowly the traveller drew from his tunic a cord from which hung a circle of gold.

"Just this ring."

"That'll do," joked Much and put out a hand. The young man's face grew dark. He reached for his sword. Robin held up a hand.

"That ring's worth a lot to you, my friend."

The young man nodded. "Seven years I've had it. It was my token... for my wedding."

"Happy man."

"Not so. Yesterday I was told that my sweetheart is to marry another, an old knight – a wealthy man – against her will."

"So that put a stop to your singing? What do they call you?"

12

"Allan-a-Dale."

"And you love this girl?"

"I do."

"What would you give if we helped you to win her again?"

The young man's face, which had brightened, now clouded just as quickly.

"I've nothing to give you. But…if you helped me I'd be your man for life, I swear, on the Book."

Robin nodded. "That's worth more than gold. Now when and where is the wedding to be."

"This very day, not five miles from here."

Robin turned to his men. "Run, get us some other gear, a long cloak and a hat. I fancy a walk to the wedding."

The church was full of guests dressed in their finery – the grandest people in the county had come. And none looked grander than the Bishop in his white and gold, as he waited in the porch.

Villagers came crowding to stare and wonder. How lovely was the bride? How old the groom? They thronged the churchyard. Nothing like this had been seen in years.

They were not disappointed. It was a wedding to remember.

As they waited for the bridal pair, a man in a feathered hat and long cloak pushed his way into the church porch. He bowed to the Bishop and spoke boldly.

"My lord, do you want music for your wedding? I play the best harp in the North Country."

The Bishop rubbed his hands. "Just what we need, my man. And what shall we pay you?"

The minstrel's keen eyes looked closely at the fat prelate. "Never mind the payment, for now. I don't play until I see the happy pair."

The Bishop smirked. "Here they come now, harper. Strike up!"

Those crowding the churchyard gate stood aside and gawped as a tall thin man with white hair and wispy grey beard, his rich grey cloak held up by two pages, approached the porch.

"Who's this then?" asked the harper. "The bride's father?"

"No, God forbid." The Bishop was shocked. "That is the groom, man. Show respect. Now here comes the bride. Hold your insolent tongue and play a tune for your pay."

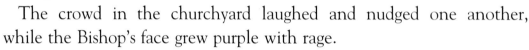

Attended by her maids, a young girl of sparkling beauty, all in white, golden hair shining, came through the gate. Her lovely face was as pale as the bridal gown, her eyes full of sorrow.

"Call that a match?" said the harper in disgust.

The crowd in the churchyard laughed and nudged one another, while the Bishop's face grew purple with rage.

"Shut your mouth and play, you rogue."

"I'll give you a tune," answered the minstrel.

Throwing back his dark cloak, he raised a green-shirted arm. Three horn blasts echoed against the stone walls of the church. With each note, the crowd grew more still, the Bishop's face more pale.

Then people ran to left and right as rank on rank of armed men in green marched into the space before the porch.

The golden-haired girl turned and called in surprise and delight.

"Allan!"

There he was, dressed once more in red and carrying a great bow. This he handed to the harper who now threw off his cloak entirely and showed himself in full Lincoln green, sword at his side.

"Robin Hood!" gasped the crowd.

Robin turned to the bride and bowed. Then he tapped Allan-a-Dale on the shoulder with his bow.

"Is this your true love and intended husband, maiden? Tell the truth and fear nought."

"It is. It is," she said. The churchyard buzzed with chatter, then with laughter, then with cheers.

Robin raised his bow and all were silent again. "Before we leave this day, you two shall be wed."

The Bishop shook with rage. "Not so. The law says that the couple shall be asked for in church three Sundays in a row."

"The law says?" returned the outlaw chief. "Well, I say we have no time for that. Ask now, three times, and make it quickly."

Though frightened, the angry Bishop stood his ground. "I'll not do it."

"Then make way for one who will." Little John stepped forward and as the crowd looked on, dumbstruck, he snatched the Bishop's robe from his back and forced it on over his own great shoulders.

"Follow me," he bellowed.

Bride, groom and all pressed into the church. Only the Bishop and the old knight were left outside, choking on their bile.

At the altar, Little John faced about. Once, twice, three times he asked if anyone would say "no" to the match. But there was silence.

"To make certain sure," the "Bishop" said, "I'll ask you seven times." And so he did.

"Who gives this bride away?" he solemnly demanded.

Robin stepped forward.

"I do." He faced the crowded church. "I, Robin Hood, give this bride. Let no man part her from her true love, Allan-a-Dale, or he will pay for it."

The wedding service ended and Robin spoke again.

"Come one, come all. Today the wedding feast's at my expense, in my green hall beneath our Trysting Tree."

THE SAD KNIGHT

Little John gazed up into the sky above the forest. The sun rode high and bright. His eyes turned to the Trysting Tree, where Robin Hood leaned against the massive trunk, deep in thought. On the grass nearby sat Will Scarlet and Much the Miller's son. They glanced at one another, grinned and said nothing.

Then the noonday silence was broken by a sound like a rolling barrel. Little John's belly was rumbling. At last the big man spoke.

"Master! If we had dinner now, you'd be all the better for it."

Now Will and Much laughed. Robin shook his head.

"You know the rule, John. First we must have a guest, baron, abbot or knight, I don't care which, as long as he has the price of our meal in his pocket. Then when our guest is here, we shall say mass, one for the Father, one for the Holy Ghost and one for our Dear Lady. And afterwards, we dine."

Little John looked up again at the sun. He spoke to himself, but everyone under the trees could hear him.

"The day's half gone. God send us a guest."

Robin smiled. "John, take your bow. Let Much and Will go with you. Walk up the Sayles as far as Watling Street. See who comes our way. You find a guest and I'll wager dinner will be ready when you come back."

Some little while later, the three outlaws stood upon the ridge above the Roman road. First they looked this way, then that. They could see a good mile in each direction. But no travellers came.

Little John's stomach growled again. The others began to chuckle, then stopped as they saw his face. Above them the sun had passed its highest point.

Much plucked at the tall man's sleeve. "Look there! Not on the high road, but that dark way out of Barnesdale. There's our guest."

"What, him?" Will Scarlet spoke, astonished.

They watched as the rider drew nearer, his horse wearily climbing the slope.

"That's a miserable guest!"

Will spoke the truth. The wayfarer, shabbily dressed, rode carelessly, one foot in the stirrup, the other hanging down. The hood had fallen over his eyes.

Little John began to stride towards the path. "Sad or not, he's a knight. He's our dinner."

Before the others could catch up, Little John had stopped in front of the horseman. The face looking down was weather-worn and battle-scarred, unafraid, but sorrowful, almost as if he had been weeping.

The huge outlaw bent his leg, one knee on the grass and threw back his hood.

"Welcome, gentle knight, welcome to greenwood."

There was no answer, simply a courteous nod.

"My master invites you to eat." And Little John added on his own account: "Dinner has been waiting these three hours."

At last the knight spoke, slowly, as if to overcome his feelings. "I was going to dine in Doncaster, or Blyth maybe. But, who is your master?"

"Robin Hood."

"Ah. I've heard much good of him. I'll come with you, willingly."

Little John rose and the three outlaws led the sad knight into the forest.

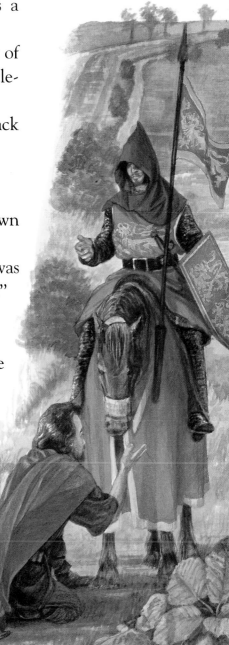

As they reached the cool shade of the mighty oak, the smell of cooking filled the air. The grass was spread with white cloths and steaming dishes, haunch of venison, roast swan and pheasant, fish. Wine and ale sparkled in flagons.

The knight dismounted and Robin Hood came forward to greet him, as Little John had done, down on one knee, his green hood thrown back.

"God save you, Robin, and all your men," said the guest.

Water and towels were brought, hands washed. Prayers were said and the meal began. For a good half hour little was said, until the sad knight broke the silence.

"It's a long time since I have eaten so well. Next time when I come this way, I must give you a meal to match this."

"What?" demanded Robin. "Should I be so greedy as to expect a meal?" He paused a moment and the outlaws smiled among themselves for they knew what he would say next.

"But, pay before you go. It is not right for a yeoman to treat a knight."

Now the traveller lowered his head. "I'm ashamed to say it, Robin, but I have nothing to pay with."

Robin turned to Little John. "Go look." Then he asked the knight, "Is that the truth?"

"I've only ten shillings."

"If that is so," went on Robin, "I will not take a penny. And, if you need more money, we'll lend it to you."

Little John whispered in the leader's ear. "The knight's true enough. There's half a pound in his strong box and no more."

"Then serve more wine," called Robin, "and make it the best. The knight shall tell his story. No wonder you're dressed so poorly. Tell me, and be sure your secret shall be kept. Did they make you become a knight to get a fee from you?"

The outlaw chief looked shrewdly at the man's unhappy face. "Or have you lost your wealth in bad living, brawling and strife, lending and borrowing?"

The sad eyes flashed with temper for a moment.

"None of these, by God that made me. My father, his father before him for a hundred years and more, have been knights. Hear me, Robin Hood – a man may be in disgrace through no fault of his. It is God's will and God will put it right in the end."

"Tell your story, then."

More wine was poured. The outlaw band listened in silence as the knight spoke, his voice low.

"My name is Sir Richard of the Lee. Two years since, my neighbours could tell you, I earned well from my estates. But then I lost all. Only my family remains."

"Lost it? How?"

"Through folly and through kindness. My son, my heir, a fine boy, twenty years old, was a great champion on the tournament field. He killed a knight and a squire.

"To pay the price for this, and save him, I had to borrow four hundred pounds."

"Who did you borrow from?" asked Robin

"From the rich Abbot of St Mary's."

"Ah, him."

"And now, the day to repay the money will soon be here. If I cannot find four hundred pounds, I will lose my castle, land and goods."

"If you cannot pay, what will you do?"

The knight's voice began to break. "I'll leave my own country and voyage to the Holy Land. I'll never return."

Sir Richard rose from table. "Farewell and thank you, Robin. There's no more to say."

Robin stood up. "Wait. Have you no friends to help you?"

"I had," answered the knight bitterly. "When I was rich, there were flocks of them. But now they run from me. They do not care to know me."

These last words brought tears to the eyes of the men in green who clustered round.

"So all you have is forfeit, just for four hundred pounds," said Robin. "Sir Richard, we shall lend you that. But who will guarantee our loan?"

The knight shrugged. "I have no name to offer, none but God in Heaven."

"Don't joke with me," Robin burst out. "God in Heaven? Why not St Peter or St Paul? Find some better guarantor, or get on the road again."

In despair, Sir Richard answered, "There is no other that I know, save our Dear Lady."

"Now we have it." Robin spoke with force. "I know of no better security in all England, than our Dear Lady."

He beckoned Little John.

"Go to our treasure chest. Count out twenty score pounds."

Little John did as he was bid. The gleaming gold coins were scooped in great handfuls and thrown down onto his wide cloak where it lay on the grass.

"Count it properly," Much told him.

Little John glared back. "Hold your mouth, Much. This is to save a good knight from poverty."

Little John brought the money to table. Then he eyed the traveller.

"See the knight's clothes, Robin. We cannot let him go like that. You've got more cloth, scarlet and green, than any merchant in England."

"Measure Sir Richard three yards of each, then," came the reply.

Little John stood up once more and began to measure cloth, using his longbow as a yardstick. With each sweep of his great hand, he added three feet of Lincoln cloth.

Much stared. "What a devil's draper you are, John."

Will Scarlet joked: "John gives good measure, Much, because it costs him nothing."

Laughing, they brought the cloth to Sir Richard and the men urged Robin: "Let him have a good horse, a grey courser, instead of that broken-down nag, and a saddle...."

Robin nodded. "And what will you give Sir Richard, Little John?"

"I'll give him a pair of shining gilt spurs, so he may think of our company and pray for us as he rides."

The knight mastered his feelings and spoke earnestly to Robin Hood. "When shall I repay you?"

"This day, twelve months from now, under this very tree," began Robin, then he paused in thought a while. "It is a shame for a knight to ride alone, without a squire. Little John will ride with you and take a yeoman's place at your right hand.

"Now, Sir Richard, fare well, and God go with you. We meet in a year's time, on this spot."

THE ABBOT
GETS HIS GOLD

In the cool gloom of his chamber sat the Abbot of St Mary's. This was a man who carried himself like a lord. His robes were grey but the cloth was rich.

Rings twinkled on his fingers as he picked up a parchment from the great oak table before him and read the script. Though faded with age, the writing was still clear. It pleased him.

There was a knock at the door and the Prior came in, slow and respectful. He had a gentle face, though his eyes were keen. And now they fell on the document in the Abbot's hands.

"Sir Richard's lands," he said.

The Abbot nodded. "Sir Richard's lands. This day twelve months ago he came to me and begged four hundred pounds in gold. And if he does not return with them today, he will lose all he owns."

Shaking his head, the Prior said, "It is a great pity a knight should lose his lands because he owes money."

He glanced at the window. "It is early yet. The day's not half gone. Perhaps he's on his way."

"Not he!" The Abbot spoke with force. "We shall see neither knight nor money. Good riddance."

The Prior raised his head to look the Abbot in the eye.

"You do him wrong. He may be over the sea, suffering hunger and cold, lying hard at night. If you take his lands it will be on your conscience."

"By God and St George!" burst out the Abbot. "Must you always be in my way?"

With these words the door opened again and the High Cellarer, a brawny monk with a huge head, entered.

"The knight is dead or hanged," he told the Abbot. "And the Abbey shall be four hundred pounds a year the better for it when we own his lands."

He bowed. "My lord, it is time to dine."

The Abbot rose and the others stood aside to let him pass. All three moved out into the arched passage and so to the Great Hall.

A lean, grey man, the Chief Justice, was waiting for them as they arrived at table. He eyed the scroll in the Abbot's hand.

"Sir Richard's deeds," said the Abbot. "If he does not bring four hundred pounds in gold today, he will be disinherited."

Casting a quick glance at the gleaming white cloth and rich spread of dishes, the justice answered, "He will not come. Let us dine."

The noonday sun shone on the city walls as a knight and his attendant, dressed gaily in red and green, rode through the gates. Their horses' hooves clattered over the cobbled streets and halted in front of the Abbey doors.

Sir Richard turned to the broad-shouldered man who rode behind him.

"Little John, before we enter, we'll change our clothes."

Quickly they dismounted and put on worn, travel-stained coats and mantles over their colourful tunics. As they were changing, the Abbey doors opened and the porter ran out, followed by stable boys. He bobbed his head to the knight.

"Welcome, good sir. My master has gone to dine. There are many gentlemen there, all waiting to see you."

His eye rested on the knight's grey courser with its bright harness.

"That's a fine horse. Quick, lead it into the stables."

"No," said the knight sharply. "The horses stay outside. We shall not linger here."

He nodded to Little John and the two went into the Abbey.

The row of dark-robed men at table looked up from their eating in astonishment as the knight, dressed in dusty brown, and his tall servant marched into the hall.

Sir Richard advanced towards the table, but paused half-way and knelt down.

"Do gladly, my lord Abbot. I have kept my word and held to my day."

The Abbot did not return the greeting. "Have you brought the gold?" he asked.

Sir Richard's answer was just as short. "Not one penny."

Turning to the Chief Justice, the Abbot raised his wine cup. "There's a shameless debtor for you."

Then to the knight, he said, "Why are you here?"

"To beg you for more time to pay," answered Sir Richard. Still on one knee, he appealed. "Sir Justice, be my friend. Protect me from those who would do me harm."

But the grey lawman only shook his head, his eyes shifting. "I owe the Abbot my loyalty. I owe him much else besides."

"Good sir Abbot," the knight tried once more. "If you will only hold my land for me while I get money to meet my debts, I will stay here and be your servant until you are paid."

Crash went the Abbot's fist upon the table. "By God you'll not get your land from me like that."

Anger filled Sir Richard at these harsh words. "By dear worthy God," he swore, "if I do not get back my lands, then someone will pay for it."

His eye swept over those at table. "A man should find out where his friends are before he is in need."

Now the Abbot stretched out an arm in fury. His look was full of loathing.

"False knight. Out from my hall and be quick."

Sir Richard leapt to his feet and replied with equal strength.

"I'm no false knight and never have been. I've risked my life and limb in combat as readily as anyone. And as for you – to make a knight kneel for so long – you have no manners."

Leaning forward hastily, the Justice put in a word. "Can you not give the knight a sum of money to let his lands go? Otherwise you will never hold them in peace."

"A hundred pounds." The Abbot's voice was grudging.

"Say two hundred," urged the Justice.

"No, by God," broke in Sir Richard. "If you gave me a thousand pounds in gold, you will never be my heirs, Abbot, Justice or Monk."

Proudly, the knight strode to the table. Behind him the silent giant bore a great bag which clinked as they approached.

"Here's the gold you lent me," the knight told the Abbot. "Had you shown any courtesy, I would have paid you something extra for the loan."

Down fell the bag among the silver dishes. Now the Abbot had lost both appetite and tongue. But not for long. He rounded on the lawman.

"You can give me back the money I gave you."

"Not a penny, by God who died on the Tree," swore the Justice.

"Sir Abbot and men of law, I've held my day," the knight spoke in triumph. "Now I shall have my land again."

Reaching across the table, he plucked up the parchment scroll, turned on his heel and, with Little John close behind him, marched from the hall.

Outside in the sunshine, they stripped off the threadbare garb that covered their scarlet and green. Throwing the dusty clothes to the porter who stood by open-mouthed, they wheeled their horses about and galloped from the city.

As the sound of hooves in the distance reached her chamber, Sir Richard's lady wife ran down to the inner gate of the castle. Beyond the courtyard the portcullis was rising in the outer wall as the mounted party rode across in colourful array.

She greeted her husband as he leapt from his horse, asking him half in hope, half in fear, "Have you lost your lands, husband? Tell me!"

He shook his head and laughed.

"No, my lady. You must pray for Robin Hood. May his soul dwell in bliss for ever. He lent me money and his best man to ride at my side.

"I have dealt with the Abbot. He has his gold. We have our home and lands."

"But you must repay Robin Hood," she said.

"True," answered Sir Richard. "But now we have time on our side."

Little John Gets His Dinner

One idle day in midsummer, Little John roamed out from Sir Richard's castle. His way took him through the meadows near the city where young men had set up the butts to show their skill with bow and arrow.

This was a chance not to be missed and Little John joined in with the rest. Three times he drew bow and three times hit the mark, the shaft piercing clean through the willow wand set up as a target.

Making ready to shoot again, the tall outlaw heard someone call in a commanding voice. He quickly recognized the richly-dressed and haughty man. It was the Sheriff of Nottingham himself.

Luckily, thought John, he does not recognize me.

"You're handy with the bow. What's your name and where do you hail from?"

Little John answered quickly, and with respect.

"My Lord, I'm from Holderness in the East. When I'm at home, men call me Reynold Greenleaf."

The Sheriff looked him over once more, then said, "Will you be my man and serve me? I'll pay you twenty marks a year."

Little John made up his mind in the blink of an eye. "I have a master, my Lord, and a gracious one, Sir Richard of the Lee. If you would only ask his leave, then I would be well pleased to serve you."

Inside himself he laughed, thinking: nothing would please me more. As I'm a true man, God help me, I'll be the worst servant a Sheriff of Nottingham ever saw.

His new master nodded. "That is well. I'll send word to Sir Richard, and from now on, you're my man."

"My lord."

Little John dropped on one knee, bending his head to hide the smile that came unbidden to his lips.

So it was done and the outlaw took up his quarters among the men-at-arms in the Sheriff's hall. All went well. His bed was comfortable, the food was plentiful. The Sheriff had a fine cook. The beer was strong. Little John ate, drank and slept well.

Too well. One morning the Sheriff and his men went hunting. The horses' hooves clopped over the courtyard, the horns sounded. But Little John was fast asleep, and because he was a new man, the others forgot to wake him.

When he rubbed the sleep from his eyes at last, the sun stood over the castle walls and his empty belly was rumbling its old tune.

He knew his way around and his feet took him, half asleep, to the steward's door.

"Good sir steward," he said winningly. "My dinner, if you please."

"What, you rogue? You have the impudence to ask for food, when your master's gone hunting? You'll eat when he gets back and not before."

"The sun will be down," protested Little John.

"It'll do you good to fast," jeered the steward.

Little John said no more but lumbered away in search of the butler. Quick as a flash that man slammed the buttery door, turned the key and barred the way.

"Nothing for you here, you idle rascal."

This time, the big man wasted no words. Out went his fist. He meant no more than a tap, but the butler felt it all the way down his back – as if it would break.

Crash! The door burst open as Little John raised his foot. Soon he was making up for lost time among the food and drink.

"What's this, you gannet?"

There came a roar from the kitchen. The cook stood in the buttery doorway, hands on hips.

"What sort of servant are you, you great lump? Helping yourself like this?"

Little John ignored him and went on eating. But in a trice he found himself lying on the floor. One blow from the cook's meaty paw sent him head over heels. Little John struggled to his feet. And down he went again.

The outlaw bellowed with laughter. Picking himself up, he shouldered the angry cook out of the way and barged out into the hall. Snatching a sword from the arms rack, he growled like a bear and went for the cook.

But this was no ordinary scullion. Nimbly the cook dodged the blade, leapt to the wall and armed himself.

Then they were at it hammer and tongs, up and down the hall, overturning the tables, rolling in the rushes, hacking and thrusting, roaring and grunting. With a clash of steel they blundered out into the courtyard. For a whole hour the battle raged. But for all their sweating and straining, neither of them could put a mark on the other.

At last Little John, gasping for breath, put up his hand.

"By God and my faith, cook. You're the best swordsman I ever saw."

The other dropped his sword point and wiped the sweat from his red face. He laughed.

"Can you shoot as well?" demanded the big man. "If so, come with me to the greenwood and be one of Robin Hood's men."

"Robin Hood?" A knowing grin came over the cook's face.

"Yes. You'll have two changes of clothes a year. Green for summer, red for winter, and twenty marks pay. What do you say?"

"I say gladly," answered the cook, leading the way back to the kitchen. There, while the other servants kept out of sight, they dined on haunch of venison, best bread and wine.

After the meal, they agreed they would be in the forest before the day was much older.

"But not empty-handed," declared the cook. Together they broke down the door of the Sheriff's strong room. Inside they helped themselves to silver plate and drinking cups, knives and spoons and three hundred pounds in gold coins.

That afternoon they joined Robin Hood under the mighty Trysting Oak.

"God save thee, Master," said the cook. "I bring greetings from the High Sheriff, who sends you these gifts and bids you be of good cheer."

Robin looked at the loot.

"By the Three," he swore, "this did not come with his good will. But now you've come, friend, you can begin by making our supper ready."

"And we shall have a guest," added Little John. For a wicked thought had come into his head.

Without another word he left the forest clearing and went swiftly by paths and tracks he knew well, up hill and down dale until he heard the sound of hoof and horn.

"Reynold Greenleaf!" The Sheriff looked down from his horse as Little John fell on one knee, pushing back his hood. "Where have you been all day?"

"God save you, Master, I've been in the forest. I looked for game. And I have seen the strangest sight."

"What sight?"

"A hart, my lord."

"What's strange in that, the forest's full of harts."

"Ah, but a green hart, Master."

"A green hart? If you're telling the truth, I must see that. Did you kill it, Reynold?"

"Oh no, my lord, for it was not alone. There was a herd of them, seven score in number in green coats. And their antlers were so sharp I dared not shoot for fear they would gore me to death."

"Lead on, Reynold!" commanded the Sheriff.

With Little John running ahead they soon out-paced the huntsmen, and leading his master by hidden ways, Little John brought him to the clearing.

There, to the Sheriff's astonishment, the space under the great oak was crowded with figures in green, all pointing and laughing.

"Woe to thee, Greenleaf. You've betrayed me!"

Little John faced about. "I swear to God that you are to blame. I was robbed of my dinner."

Now Robin stepped forward and, full of courtesy, greeted the Sheriff.

"You shall have your supper, good sir. Be seated at our table. For love of Little John you shall have good cheer and ride safely away. Have no fear."

The Sheriff, unwilling, had no choice. He got down from his horse which was led away. As he sat down and saw the gleaming cloth, the silver dishes, he said with a groan to Little John, "Greenleaf, you have betrayed me twice. For those are my dishes."

"Nay, thrice, my lord," grinned the big outlaw. "For your meal is made by your own cook."

"Be easy at our board, sir," urged Robin Hood. "Tonight you shall lodge with us, under the trees and the stars."

At a word from Robin, the outlaws helped the Sheriff out of his fine mantle, his fur-edged kirtle, leaving only his breeches and shirt.

"Give him a green cloak," he commanded. "You shall lie in the same suit as we. Be of good cheer, for this is our order when in the greenwood."

"It's a harder order than any friar or hermit," complained the Sheriff. "I would not dwell here for all the gold in England."

"You shall live with us for twelve months," Robin told him. "You shall learn to be an outlaw."

The night passed and in the morning the Sheriff got up, his body stiff and aching. "I cannot stay another night here in the greenwood," he declared. "Robin Hood, I pray you, rather than stay here I'd have you strike my head off my shoulders. Let me go, for charity's sake."

Robin gave no answer and the Sheriff spoke again. "Let me go and I will be the best friend that ever you and your men had."

The outlaw chief took out his sword and held it up so the blade flashed in the early morning sun.

"Then swear an oath on this bright brand, that you will never seek to harm me, by water or land. And if you find any of my men, by night or day, you'll serve them well. Swear, upon your honour, swear!"

Little John muttered to Robin. "Save your breath. He'll never keep his word."

Robin answered, "Let that be on his conscience then." Turning to the Sheriff, he said again, "Swear!"

The Sheriff could not say no. He swore his oath. Then his fine clothes were brought back to him, his horse led up and, mounted again, he rode off as fast as it could carry him, down the forest ways towards Nottingham town. As he rode he picked the scraps of leaf and twig from his sleeves and brooded on what had been done to him.

A DEBT REPAID

A year had passed and outside Sir Richard's castle gate gathered a hundred horsemen. All dressed in red and white, they made a brave show.

Each one carried a bow well strung and from each belt hung a quiver with yard-long arrows, tips burnished, and flighted not with dull grey goose but bright peacock feathers, and trimmed with silver.

The gates rumbled back. The knight, finely-harnessed, rode out. Behind his courser trotted a pack-horse led by a footman. On its back was strapped a great trunk and inside the chest lay four hundred pounds in gold.

Raising a gloved hand, Sir Richard called, "To Barnesdale!" and the colourful party set off down the road. By noon they were well on their way. The knight began to think of the forest ahead, the outlaw band and Robin Hood, picturing his face as he saw the beggar knight return to repay his loan, and bringing lavish gifts. As they rode they heard tremendous shouting ahead. Their way led through a sweeping meadow thronged with folk. Right in the middle was a roped square where men, stripped to the waist, rolled and tumbled.

"A wrestling match, sir," said the squire. "May we stop to see it?"

"We must be with Robin Hood before the end of day," returned the knight. Then he looked up at the sun and said, "Maybe for an hour."

His men nudged one another and pointed. "See the prizes," said one. "A white bull."

"A courser with saddle and bridle," said another.

"A pipe of wine, red-gold gauntlets," added a third. "O lucky winner."

33

"Maybe not," thought Sir Richard as his party reached the edge of the throng.

A yeoman, tall and strong, clearly the winner, was hemmed in by a jostling mob. But they were not cheering. There were cries of hate and anger. The victor was pushed and pulled. In another moment he would be felled and trampled underfoot.

"What's this?" shouted Sir Richard above the din. "The man won fairly, didn't he?"

Faces turned in the crowd. A man answered, "He's none of us. He's a stranger, a forren."

Suddenly the young man fell to the ground. A menacing howl went up. "Kill him!"

For a second Sir Richard hesitated. This was not his affair. He was a traveller passing through. But in that moment, into his mind came another picture, the lean tanned face of the outlaw Robin Hood.

"Forward," he yelled and spurred his horse. Massing together, his men ploughed into the furious crowd.

Little John looked at the sky, then at his master leaning against the broad trunk of the Trysting Tree.

"Let's go to dinner," he urged.

Robin shook his head. "No. Today, I should have had my four hundred pounds returned. Our Lady must be angry with me, for she has not sent my pay."

"The sun's not down, yet," urged Little John. "Trust the knight. But meantime, Master, you must be hungry."

Robin eyed the tall man. "Take your bow, then, and go up to Watling Street with Will and Much. See if anyone is coming."

"Anyone?"

"Aye, traveller, messenger, someone with a tale to tell. Or a poor man with nothing, someone we can help from our store."

Grumbling to himself, John buckled on his sword and the three went up to the ridge above the road.

For a while no one came, though they spied east and west. But at last Much pointed. "Look there, on the forest track."

A dark-robed monk came riding on a palfrey. But not alone, for after him ambled pack-horses, a groom, a page boy, and behind them armed men, two by two.

John grinned. "I'll wager they've brought our money. Bows ready, lads, stand fast."

"He looks like a monk," said Will, "but he rides as royally as a bishop. Seven pack-horses and two... four... six," he counted, "nigh fifty men-at-arms."

"And we no more than three," retorted John. "Well, bend your bow. I have the monk's crown in my sight."

He looked more closely now. The cowled figure on the leading horse had a massive head. Hadn't he seen this churchman before?

Stepping into the track, bow curved, arrow notched, he called: "Hold. Not a step more, monk. Or by dear worthy God, there's bad luck for you at the end of this arrow.

"Hold!" he cried again. "My master's angry with you. You've kept him waiting for his dinner."

Now the monk reined in his palfrey. "Who's your master?" he demanded pompously.

"Robin Hood."

"Oh, that thief. I've heard no good of him."

"You lie and you'll be sorry for it," returned the outlaw. "He's a yeoman of the forest and he's invited you to dine."

The monk stared, then abruptly turned about to call up his men. Then gawped again. For only the groom, the little page and the pack-horses were to be seen. The men-at-arms had melted away into the forest bushes.

Willing or not, the monk with the great head was led to Robin Hood's lodge. The outlaw chief greeted him, courteous as ever. But the guest kept his hood on.

"He's a churl, by God," muttered Little John.

"No matter," answered Robin. "He's never learnt manners. Say, how many men did this traveller have with him?"

"Some fifty-two when first we met."

"Then sound the horn," ordered Robin, "lest they should dare to return."

To the monk's stupefaction, the clearing suddenly crowded with seven score young men in green, armed and ready.

"Bring water for washing. We shall eat."

Soon the meal was underway. "Do gladly, sir monk," Robin told him. "What abbey are you from?"

More at ease with good food inside him, the monk answered: "St Mary's. I am just a humble servant. I am the High Cellarer."

At this, Little John looked more closely at their guest, then grinned to himself as he remembered where he had last seen him.

"The best wine," called Robin. "The monk shall drink."

Genially, the High Cellarer raised cup to lip, then stopped as Robin went on to say, "This is a great marvel. I thought Our Lady was angry with me. She was the surety for that little sum of four hundred pounds I lent the sad knight. If you, monk, are the bearer of that money on her behalf, then pray let me see it."

Robin's face was serious. The monk was alarmed.

"I – I know nothing of your loan!"

"That cannot be," Robin told him. "For God is a righteous man and so is his Lady. You told me yourself that you are the humble servant of St Mary. You serve her every day. So you must be her messenger. You have come here upon the very day appointed to repay me. Now, good monk, how much is there in the chest on your first pack-horse?"

"Some twenty marks, no more," gabbled the monk.

"We shall see." Robin signalled to his second in command. "If that's the truth, why, you must be short of money and I will lend you more. I don't want to take your spending money. Now say, Little John, how much? Does the monk tell the truth?"

In front of the gaping crowd in green, Little John tipped out the great trunk onto his open cloak where it lay on the grass. The coins cascaded down in a rush of clinking gold.

Much and Will began to count. Voices rose to the trees.

"One hundred, two hundred, three, four...." Till at last, Little John himself cried: "Eight hundred, Robin. The monk is true enough. Our Lady has doubled your cast!"

"What did I tell you?" Robin looked warmly at the guest who now sat, head sunk on his chest. "If I searched all England through I would never have found a better guarantor for my loan than our Lady Mary."

He called again. "More wine, the best. And, when you leave, sir monk, greet your Gracious Lady. If she ever needs Robin Hood he will be her true friend. If she needs silver, come to me. Now, Little John, look in the other boxes."

"By Our Lady," moaned the High Cellarer, "this is no courtesy, to bid me dine, then rob me of all I have."

"No, no," Robin assured him. "It's our custom to leave a little behind."

The monk was struggling to his feet. "I must be on my way."

"Another flagon before you go?"

"No, by God." The monk stumbled to his palfrey and struggled into the saddle. "I could have dined in Doncaster or Blyth much cheaper than at your table."

As he rode away, his servants running after him, Robin called, "My greetings to your Abbot. May he send me a monk like you every day!"

The laughter died down. But now Robin lost interest in the food and drink. Shadows were lengthening through the trees as the sun began to lower in the sky. He had his money, but he had thought the knight would keep his word.

Then the lookout called. "Men-at-arms approaching. A hundred of them."

Robin sprang up and bid his men stand ready. Now he advanced to the edge of the clearing to look down at the cavalcade advancing up the forest slope. Straightaway he recognized the knight.

"God save you, knight, and welcome."

"God save you, Robin and all your company." Sir Richard leapt from his horse and came towards them.

"Why so long?"

"Robin, first let me speak. Though the Abbot and Chief Justice would have taken my land, thanks to God and you, they never got it. But do not be displeased with me for keeping you waiting. On our way we came on a wrestling match. The winner, a yeoman, was about to be slain as a stranger. For your sake, Robin, I and my men pushed into the press and rescued him. Then I paid for five barrels of wine to make all well. That delayed me."

"By God," said Robin, "whoever helps a yeoman is my friend."

He looked at Sir Richard's followers.

"What are these bows and arrows with peacock feathers and all?"

"A gift for you and your men, Robin. And here in my chest are the four hundred pounds in gold I owe you. And twenty marks for your kindness."

Robin laughed. "Be of good cheer, sir knight. And keep your coin. I've no need of it."

"No need?" The knight was astonished.

"Our Lady sent her High Cellarer to repay your loan. I should not be so greedy as to expect it repaid twice.

"Now, Little John," he said, "bring the other four hundred of the monk's treasure. I do not need the extra. The knight shall have it. Buy horse and harness, Sir Richard, and gild your spurs again. And if you ever need money, come back to Robin Hood. But use your four hundred pounds and make sure that never again you'll be in such need."

"I thank you, Robin," answered the knight. "And for my part I'll say, if ever you have need of help, then come to my gate."

With that all sat down again to eat and drink.

ROBIN'S DREAM

In the dark time before the dawn of spring, Robin Hood was plagued with a dream.

He walked alone on a deep forest track. In front of him two men appeared – a little way off but moving ever closer. They were dressed in colours of autumn. Not the bright flame of the silver birch but the sombre hues of the beech, under whose shade no flower grows.

One pointed at Robin, the other advanced on him. He was a yeoman, powerful in body, dressed from his head to his heel in horse hide with mane and tail. His sword and dagger gleamed in the gloom of the forest.

Robin strove to move and to resist but his limbs would not let him fight, nor would they let him flee.

They seized and bound him. They began to beat him. Blows thudded on his head and shoulders. Arms and legs were wracked with pain and his body's strength ebbed away.

Slowly he began to fall into darkness.

Then he woke in the pale daybreak. Above him were the laced boughs of the lodge. Around him were the smells of wood-smoke and cooking meat and the sounds of his comrades stirring.

"What is it, Master?" asked Little John, and Robin slowly recalled his nightmare.

"Dreams come and go," the tall man told him. "Dreams are like wind on the hill. No matter how hard they blow at night, in the morning it will be calm and still."

Robin nodded. Little John spoke wisely. He rose and put on his green jacket and his sword belt. In the bright morning of the greenwood, he forgot the dream.

But deep within him, its shadow lurked.

THE FRIAR OF FOUNTAINDALE

Robin's men were at practice in Sherwood. Beneath the spreading arms of the Trysting Oak, they set up willow stems as markers, topped with a garland of leafy twigs. Turn and turn about they shot. Some arrows missed, some struck the garland. Others slit clean through the willow wand, to the cheers of the rest.

Little by little the mark was shifted further off – three hundred feet, then four hundred. As the distance grew, more archers dropped out until the five hundred mark was reached.

By this time only Will Scarlet, Much the Miller's Son, Gilbert White Hand and Little John were left. One by one they shot, all within the garland, till at last Robin's right-hand man let go a bolt that burst the wand in three.

A great yell went up to the forest curtain above them and Robin laughed.

"I'm blessed by God and that is so. I could ride a hundred miles from here and never find better archers, better huntsmen than you."

As the cheers died down again, Will said with a smile, "No need to ride a hundred miles, or a score even, Robin. You can find one who'll beat all comers here."

Robin was amazed. "And who would that be? Why have I not met him?"

"The curtal friar of Fountaindale."

"A friar?" Robin laughed again with contempt.

"No ordinary friar," said Will. "He lives on his own and bows to no one, earl, abbot or knight. Seven years he's lived there and no one can command him."

"This friar I shall see," said Robin.

"This friar we must all see," added Little John.

Robin turned. "I shall go alone. You may all follow close behind, but when we come to Fountaindale, you shall stay hid." He chuckled. "I don't want a crowd of sinners to alarm the holy man."

The band set out and in a couple of hours, before the sun had topped the sky, they came on a broad stretch of grassy ground through which a wide stream wandered. It was a quiet and pleasant spot.

At a sign from Robin, the outlaws hid themselves in the bushes at the edge of the meadow, while he went forward to the water, whistling as he walked.

He smiled to himself at the thought of a fighting friar, but he took no chances. His bow was at his back, his quiver by his side. From the broad belt hung both sword and dagger, over one arm was a buckler, and instead of a hood he wore a round steel cap.

Just as he reached the bank, a figure rose suddenly from behind a willow clump. Robin was taken aback at the sight.

Here was a friar right enough. His corpulent body with its curving belly was clad in a brown robe, tucked up at the knee to show brawny bare legs and huge feet in sandals. Around his head was a fringe of thick brown hair. But sitting on top of the tonsure was a helmet as bright as Robin's. And around his waist was no cord but a leather belt, with sword and dagger. A buckler likewise covered his left forearm.

"*Pax vobiscum*, my son," the friar greeted him. "Peace be with you."

Robin's mouth began to shake, but he hid his smile.

"Good friar," he said winningly, "I'm a weary traveller. Will you carry me over the water for Charity's sake?"

The burly friar looked him over. "Well, it is some days since I did a good deed. Come, climb on my back."

He bent down. Robin, delighted, looked quickly back to the bushes where his men were hidden, then sprang up, clasped the friar round the neck and the holy man waded into the water. By the time they had gone a half dozen paces, he had to hitch his skirts higher. Puffing and grunting, he advanced until he reached the shallows, then set Robin down on the sedge.

Robin looked across the stream again. So far so good. But what next? The next move was the friar's and took him by surprise.

"My son, one good deed calls for another. Now carry me back over the brook."

Robin looked at the friar's deep chest and vast paunch, the mighty thighs, and thought of that weight on his back.

But before he could refuse, the friar put a hand on his sword hilt. "Or as sure as you're a bold outlaw you'll feel the length of this."

It was ferry or fight. Robin saw the joke, bent down and next moment felt his spine buckle as the gross friar sprang like a goat and landed on him.

Down they went into the current. Robin's feet were forced into the mud below until he could scarcely drag his legs forward. Soon he was in up to his thighs and every limb in his strong body groaned.

At last he struggled up the bank again, back where he had begun. All was quiet around him. He did not look up this time, but he knew the bushes were crowded with grinning outlaws. This would not do.

"I must be on my way, friar. Enough is enough. Carry me over one time more, or you'll have a taste of my sword edge."

To his astonishment, the fat friar said nothing but bent his massive

back, took him on board and plunged in, forging through the deeper water until it rose almost to his hips. Then, when they had reached the very middle, Robin felt a sudden shock. The friar ducked down and he flew over the steel-capped head into the water with a great splash.

Blowing mud and weed from his mouth, Robin scrambled out on to the bank. But fast as he moved, the portly friar, robes dripping wet, was out on the bank at the same time.

Snatching the bow from his back, Robin notched an arrow swift as light and loosed it at the grinning priest. But swifter still the plump arm rose and the buckler sent the arrow spinning harmlessly away.

More speedy still, Robin shot again, and a third time. But, laughing, the fat man knocked the shots aside.

"Do better, my son. I don't care a toss for your pins and needles."

Irked, Robin dropped his bow, slid out his sword and with buckler covering his left forearm, he rushed the friar.

"I'll give you good deeds, Father!"

"Come to me, outlaw!" was the answer.

The quiet vale rang and clanged like a smithy on market day as metal struck metal. The blades thrust and jarred, slashed and hacked. But quick as Robin darted and lunged, the stout man in the robe skipped nimbly this way and that, parried each blow with his buckler and made Robin jump with the whirring blade.

The sun had passed its noon height and still they fought on. Though his face was scarlet the fat man showed no signs of weakening.

At last Robin dropped his sword point. "A boon, sir friar," he gasped.

"Ask," snorted the friar. "Do you yield? Will you do penance?"

"No, I just wish to blow my little horn."

The friar cackled. "Blow if you please. Blow till your eyes pop out for all I care."

Robin blew and at once the bushes on the borders of the meadow came to life as fifty men in green swarmed down to the bank. The friar watched them, eyes bulging.

"Well blown. If that's your game, then I must have a boon. Let me whistle."

"Till your cheeks burst," jeered Robin.

Up went the fat fingers. There was an ear-splitting shriek. From the distance came a racket of barking and snarling and down the slope rushed a great pack of bandogs, lips curled back to show slavering teeth.

Without a moment's pause they went for the outlaws, ripping jackets and tunics.

Those who could, drew bow and shot. But as fast as the arrows flew the dogs leapt up and caught the shafts between their teeth.

The friar roared with laughter. "Who blew best then, outlaw? Will you cry for mercy?"

His answer came from Little John who drew bow again.

"Call off your dogs, holy man, before I call them off for good."

As the friar made no answer, Little John let slip two arrows so quickly they were like one. The first was caught between the nearest dog's teeth, but the second caught that dog clean through the gullet and stretched the beast out on the grass.

Now the friar's red face was paler.

"Hold, hold, there's a good lad," he pleaded and whistled to his dogs.

Before the shrill sound faded, the dogs, as one, crouched down on the ground where they were. Robin signalled to his band to put up their bows.

"Good friar," he spoke warmly, "why not join us? Take new orders in a fresh parish. Come to the greenwood. Your fee will be a noble and every Holy Day you shall have new clothes. What do you say?"

The friar raised his hand.

"My blessing upon you all, brothers," he intoned.

"And what do they call you?" asked Robin.

But before he answered, Will Scarlet pointed to the holy man's water-stained robes looped round his sturdy knees.

"Tuck, tuck," he shouted. "Friar Tuck."

And the outlaws chorused: "Friar Tuck!"

A MAY PROCESSION

Dark days were past and the snow fled from the dales. Streams loosed from ice and flowers burst among the bushes. Sherwood shaws were thick with white. Not the white of snow but hawthorn blossom. May time had come back.

One morning while the woods were in half-light, Little John woke Robin in his lodge. His eyes were wary. He put a finger to his lips and raised both hands, all ten fingers out. "Foresters moving past. Ten, a score maybe. They went one by one, heading south."

Robin pulled on his jacket, took bow and sword. But even before he was ready to move, a dozen others, tried and trusted men, were waiting. Friar Tuck's fat face, heavy with sleep, was among them.

Without a word they moved through the trees, picking up the trail. Something was afoot to bring the Sheriff's woodmen to this part of the forest so early. And what concerned the verderers concerned Robin's men. The forest was theirs, whatever the Sheriff might think.

They had been on the way but a little while when Much put a finger to his ear. All stopped and listened, then nodded to one another.

From the open pasture beyond the forest fringes came the faint sound of horns, not urgent like hunters, but a chorus as if many blew together. And now the sound came closer.

Robin looked at Little John. Now the matter became clearer. They put on speed, loping down the forest tracks, but still silently, without the snap of broken twigs to alert the men they followed.

Little John, in the lead, raised a hand and stood stock still. Now he pointed ahead. Robin joined him. Again they looked at one another and nodded.

Fifty yards away the ride opened into a clearing, a dip in the ground, like a huge shallow bowl, bordered with ash and birch in spring leaf and fringed with hawthorn bushes, white as lace.

From the meadow land further off, the horns trumpeted more loudly. People were calling, whistling, laughing. Wheels creaked and, above all, shrill piping and the thump of drums.

The din grew, outside. But in the clearing all was quiet. Even the birds had stopped singing and the small creatures of the greenwood had fled.

It seemed the glade was empty. But outlaw eyes could pick out the men hidden behind thicket and tree trunk. There were twenty foresters, armed with staff and whip.

Robin signalled and the lads in green moved in closer. Now watchers were watched.

The approaching noises were deafening: horn, pipe and drum vying with laughter and the lowing of oxen.

Through the line of trees dividing forest from meadow six men came walking, green smocks striped with yellow, hats decorated with flowers. They moved with a purpose and one carried a great axe. Close behind them lumbered a wagon drawn by a dozen oxen, broad horns covered with garlands.

Around and after them swarmed a great assembly, all in green, white and yellow; youths and girls, old men and women, chattering, singing, while in and out of the throng jigged the pipers and drummers.

As the open space brimmed with folk, all noise ceased. The axeman raised his free hand.

A young woman stepped forward, her fair hair shining in the morning sun. The outlaws looked more closely. She was a beauty, a fresh and lively face. Another girl, dark as she was fair, stood at her right side.

The first girl's voice rose in the quiet. "We choose our May Tree."

Quickly she ran forward and slipped a ribbon round the trunk of a tall tree at the edge of the forest space. The axeman strode after, blade upraised.

But as he did, a rough voice from the thickets called, "Hold!"

The crowd stood still, breath held back, as a score of foresters, staves and whips at the ready, sprang from cover. A broad-shouldered bearded man spoke again.

"What do you want here?"

The axe was lowered, the ribbon slipped from the tree. The axeman answered humbly.

"Good sir. We're here to take our May bough. It's our custom."

"Your custom maybe. But you know the law, the King's law. None may take green from his forest, without his leave."

The villager looked round fearfully at the crowd behind him, then at the ring of brawny Sheriff's men, sticks and thongs in their fists. All waited for his answer. He spoke slowly in a small voice.

"But one tree, once a year."

"One too many," the chief forester replied. "And what is more, it is forbidden to trespass in the woods in summer. All forest ways are closed while the hinds cast their young."

The fair-haired girl called mockingly, "Woodman, don't lie! The hinds have not dropped their young and you know it. You make the law to suit yourself."

She turned to the axeman, like a queen.

"Strike, Dickon. Fear not. Right's on our side." She laughed. "They're no more than twenty."

A roar of delight came from the young folk by the wagon and the chief forester's face was dark with rage.

"Set to, lads."

As one, the Sheriff's men rushed in, sticks whirling. As they began, the axeman and his fellows turned and ran, each his own way. The crowd packed into the far end of the clearing were not so free. Older ones tried to struggle away. Younger ones tried to rush forward.

"Dickon, come back," the girl called.

But Dickon with the axe, and his mates, were out of sight and sound.

"Go. All of you, or we'll dust your backs," roared the forester.

"Stand fast!" shrilled the fair-haired girl.

47

They lunged at her now, sticks raised.

In the thicket, Robin whistled and from all sides the lads in green charged. Surprised, the Sheriff's men stopped in their tracks and in that instant felt the thud and smart of blows on their own flesh and bones. Half of them went head over heels on the grass.

Now the Sheriff's men fought back and the outlaws were outnumbered.

"Swords!" commanded Robin and blades leapt from scabbards.

The flash of steel was enough. The foresters broke and ran, dodging among the bushes, urged on by blows on back and buttocks. In a moment the clearing was empty of them leaving the village folk and Robin's men in possession.

"We thank you, good sir." The fair girl spread her green and yellow skirt and curtsied.

Robin bowed. "Welcome to greenwood. Be pleased to take your May Bough, fair maid."

She took up the axe where Dickon had dropped it and held out the haft.

"Be pleased to cut for us, kind sir."

Laughing, Robin swung the axe to the tree. With the first blow to the trunk, the glade rang again with shouts, the sound of horns, the screech of pipe and the roll of the drum.

Soon it was done. The May Tree lay roped to the cart, festooned with branches of aspen and birch, sprays of hawthorn and broom. Whips cracked, the flower-decked oxen put their shoulders against the yoke and the wheels groaned. As noisily as they had come, the village folk were leaving the forest.

Now the fair-haired girl and her companion, smiling, turned to the men in green. "I am Marian. This is Jinny. Will you be with us this May Day, good friends?"

"Robin," said Will Scarlet warily, "have a care. The Sheriff's men will be in the town."

Marian laughed.

"Who cares for them? Today's our day. Today May King and May

Queen rule. And we shall be masked, if you are shy. Come," she said, and her voice was a command.

"Give leave to go, Robin." The brown-robed friar stepped forward, eyes on both girls at once. "If the May Queen commands, we must obey. But tell us," he addressed the girl, "who's the Summer King today."

"Who was?" she answered. "Dickon, who carried the axe. But he'll not reign today. A king may not run away. Come, join us," she urged them.

Little John's face was eager. "Will there be food and drink?"

"Meat, bread, spiced pastries, best ale, brewed for May. All you can eat and drink and welcome."

"And dancing?" added Much.

"Dancing, games and singing as long as the sun's in the sky and you can stand on your feet."

"Come lads, we'll go." Robin led the way. All ran to catch up with the lumbering cart and its rowdy escort.

ROBIN, THE SUMMER KING

As the procession drew near, people ran from the town. Bells jangled, pipes skirled, horns bellowed and over all thundered the drums. Green ribbons streamed from hats and sleeves, screaming children ran waving sprigs of May blossom. The ox cart with its great heap of green was swallowed up in the rout, and singing, laughter and music were swallowed up in one great roar of celebration.

Yard by yard the wagon headed for the middle of the town. Following behind, Robin's men were greeted with flowers and thumps on the back. The story of the forest ambush had gone before them.

At last the throng swelled from the narrow streets into the open place before the church. Near its high sandstone walls, lodges made of branches had gone up and in front of them were long rows of tables piled with food. A huge barrel stood hard by the church gate.

The tumult grew as the May tree was rolled from the wagon and stepped up, held aloft by ropes and blocks. The square was covered in the green, white and yellow of spring.

Now the cry went up: "A ring, a ring, a chain, a chain,"

Robin's hand was seized by the fair girl, Marian. Jinny, the dark one, grabbed Tuck's arm. Little John was pulled in, then Much and the others. To pipe and drum the crowd began to swing into a long twisting line, young and old following on. It wound like a serpent round and round the square. Piper and drummer jigged up and down. Lads rushed into the middle capering and turning somersaults.

Slowly the line stretched until it had the centre space. Those not dancing drew back to walls and fences, filling the windows of the houses round.

At first it seemed the dance would last until the dancers tired. But, led by Marian, it edged to the churchyard. Legs flying, knees throwing up her skirts, Marian drew the tail of folk behind her like thread from a spinning wheel until it passed through the gate and into the yard before the church door.

There was no call, no signal, but like magic the revellers had divided, men in one line, women in another. A voice called above the clamour on pipe and tabor.

"Sovereigns all in same, come and see our game.

Pray you in God's name, dance 'ere you pass."

Round and round went the dance, higher and higher screamed the pipes, drums roared until the stone walls of the church throbbed and shook.

Then all was quiet. The hot air, scented with crushed leaves and flowers, was heavy and still.

In the silence a girl began to sing. At first she sang slowly and the great rings began to turn again in time with her words. But now no pipe played, no drum beat. Only her voice, then the answering chorus. Her voice gained pace as feet moved faster.

"Maiden in the woods lay, seven nights, seven nights.

Maiden in the woods lay, seven nights and a day."

As the women's circle and the men's flowed round, they moved in and out, towards each other and away.

"Well was her bed, what was her bed? Red rose and a red rose;

Well was her bed, what was her bed? Red rose and a violet."

Louder and swifter, turning and swaying, until the girl sang:

"Well was her love, who was her love? May King and a May King;

Well was her love, who was her love? May King in the Greenwood."

The chain came to rest. Opposite Robin stood Marian.

"May King!" cried a voice.

"May King!" answered all.

Reaching forward, Marian grasped Robin's hand and drew him to the high church wall. There stood two seats cut from oak logs. She pulled him with her until both were seated.

"May King, May Queen! Robin, Marian!" The clamour made the air shake.

Jinny stepped forward. In her hands were two garlands of willow twined with marsh-marigolds and cowslips. She held them out. Friar Tuck took them and held them aloft.

Now all was still. Tuck's unctuous voice reached beyond the churchyard into the hot square outside.

"In the name of our King and Queen in Heaven," he intoned, "I crown you, Robin, and you, Marian, May King and May Queen, Lord and Lady of the Summer. Peace and plenty attend you."

Cheers rang out. Piper and drummer set to again. But Tuck had not finished. He advanced to the railings and mounted a stone until his portly figure rose in full view.

"Brothers, sisters," he cried. "This is our chosen day, when wrong is put right and that which was divided is made one again.

"While our Lord and Lady rule, none shall suffer harm or loss."

He was silent a moment, then: "None shall be hanged or blinded for hunting the deer or for driving them out of the fields. None shall be chastised for taking the green of the forest. There shall be one law for all and justice shall not be bought and sold.

"Prelates who preach poverty and live in sinful luxury shall be cast down and those who speak truth shall be lifted up.

"So be it."

"Amen," the crowd spoke with one breath.

"Now, come one, come all and eat and drink. Here shall be no penny loaves, but only tenpenny loaves. Here shall be drunk no small beer but only strong ale. Set to."

Tuck turned, his eyes twinkling.

"Now her chaplain shall salute the queen."

He leaned towards Marian but was headed off by dark-haired Jinny.

"The friar may kiss the handmaid. Come."

She dragged him off to the tables, now swarming with folk, while in the square, crowds cavorted to pipe and drum. Robin and Marian sat down together. She gave him a long look then raised a cup.

"Long may you live, majesty."

"Long may you live, my lady," he answered.

They kissed and turned to eat. But in a little while her eye was on him again. Her voice was solemn.

"You live free in the forest, Robin. So I would live, too."

He shook his head.

"There are no maids with us. When the time is right our young men go to their loves by night. Secretly they go and secretly return."

"Why no maids in the greenwood?"

"What?" he gazed at her. "That's no maiden law to live like thieves, bow in hand, ready to shoot."

"I could live so," she said. "I'm not afraid."

Her bold answer silenced him a while. But then he told her:

"This is an outlaw's life. A man may take and kill you if he can, hang you without pity and leave your body swinging in the wind. For fear of that, no woman can live with us."

Her eyes shone.

"They say maids are weak. But if they choose they can be strong."

Warily he shook his head.

"When the sun shines all is well. But after heat comes cold, wet follows dry. Snow and frost in place of warm winds. We lie on the grass with only a roof of boughs."

Now she was angry.

"You think I only care for dancing in the streets. Well, I tell you that I can suffer what any man will stand. I'd cut my hair, loop up my skirt...."

But Robin did not hear her words. His glance was not on her, but reached beyond the crowded square to the shadowy corner by the church tower.

There, in a narrow space apart from the throng, two men stood, still and threatening.

One was a knight in russet brown and one a yeoman, armed and clad in horse hide, mane and tail.

THE OUTLAWS RETREAT

"What is it Robin?" Marian spoke. "Have I offended you?"

"No, Marian," he replied. "Look by the tower. Those two who stand there, knight and yeoman, both in brown when all the world's in green. Who are they?"

She glanced swiftly and as swiftly turned back. "That is Sir Roger, priest of this parish. He dresses always in a sombre red. Some call him Red Roger. He's a cold priest. He hates our revels but he dare not say no to us, even when we crown our Summer King in the churchyard. We have done that every spring, long before he came here – and will do it after he has gone. Don't give him a thought, Robin."

"But, what of the other man, the yeoman?"

Again she looked and this time said, "Yeoman? I see no yeoman, Robin, only our priest and now he has gone. Come," she urged him. "Forget what you saw and what you thought you saw. Eat and drink like Little John and rejoice like Friar Tuck."

Across the table, Tuck held with one hand a great cup of ale; the other arm was round Jinny's shoulders. Between gulps he sang:

"*In nomine domine,*

Sweetheart, pity me."

John gnawed at the meat bone in his fist and glared across at Tuck. "What a devil's priest you are! All seven deadly sins at once."

Tuck answered calmly, "Only those who sin know how to forgive. Go thy ways, my son."

All laughed, joined hands round the table and sang.

But as the song began, so it faltered and fell. The silence spread along the board and from table to table. Heads turned to the church tower. In the square beside it, space was made as people hurried away.

There stood the knight in dark red again, arm outstretched. And with him with were three men-at-arms, sword in hand, the badge of the Sheriff on their tabards. For a moment they held back and then began to come forward, the crowd giving way before them.

Tuck pulled his arm from Jinny's waist and lumbered up from table. Little John was on his feet, Much and Will with him, overturning the bench as they stood.

Half a dozen men in green pressed forward. Now the crowd made way for them until the two parties met in mid-square.

With a rasp, Little John drew his sword. Tuck's followed, then the others. At first the men-at-arms made as if to meet the challenge. But when the two sides were no more than two yards apart, they backed away.

Robin's men moved forward more swiftly. Now the Sheriff's soldiers turned and ran. And they were gone, full pelt round the corner of the church. Little John, Tuck and the rest sheathed their blades and swaggered back to table, sat down and went back to their eating and drinking.

But, as swiftly, Robin was on his feet.

"Little John, Tuck, Much, Will, Gilbert," he called them by name and everyone looked at him above their half-emptied plates.

"Finish your meal and quickly," he commanded.

Little John made a protest. "Finish? Why, we've scarce begun. What courtesy is that, Master?"

"Do as I say." Robin spoke sharply. "We must all be gone from here and quickly."

"What?" asked Tuck. "To leave your subjects when you're newly-crowned, Robin? That's no noblesse."

"This is no joke, good friends. We must be away to greenwood."

Little John stood. "What's amiss, Robin?"

Robin pointed to the church. "The Sheriff's men."

"Them? Poltroons. They ran. You saw them. Besides, they were three, we were twelve."

"Yes, and before another hour they'll be back, half a hundred strong."

The big man laughed. "Our good fortune. If you think odds of five to one frighten us, Robin...."

"I know that you and the rest will fight ten times your number. I am not afraid."

"There are a thousand round us," said Much. "The odds are on our side."

"No, you are wrong, Much. Some will fight and some will fly and some will fall and all will be confusion. The Sheriff's men will kill and care not who they strike, to have a chance of taking us. But if they come and find us gone, they dare not strike."

"So folk will say we ran away?" demanded John.

"Folk will say what they will. But they shall not say we hazarded their lives as well as our own. So we shall go."

With regret, Tuck struggled up from table.

"Robin is right and we shall follow him. He never failed you yet. Come, lads, kiss the maids farewell."

He flung out both arms to bless all present.

"We'll see you all when spring returns."

Then he began to sing:

"*In nomine domine,*

Sweet maid, pity me."

Marian stood by Robin. "Let me come with you."

But he shook his head. "Sweet Marian, it may not be. I dare not take you. It is not our law."

Her face was dark as he kissed her.

"Farewell, Marian."

She said not a word, but looked after Robin as he led his men away.

DUEL IN
THE FOREST

That night men went to their beds in silence. Little John was angry. Friar Tuck knew it was no use to speak words of sweet reason, for no one would listen.

At dawn, Robin got up early and roamed away into the greenwood. He did not return that night, nor the next. It was said he had a secret place, a cave or a small lodge of timber somewhere in Barnesdale. There he stayed by himself seeing no one.

After three days he came back to Sherwood. Little John put his anger on one side. The others forgot. The sun shone, the deer ran and the arrow flew.

But Robin did not join in. He ate together with his men, then walked away into the forest. The others shrugged and went to their sport, their wrestling, hunting and patrolling the greenwood to keep the foresters at a distance.

Robin roved and said nothing, choosing the loneliest paths where no bird sang and the air was still.

All the same, one morning he met a stranger. It was by chance and took him off his guard. He strode head on chest and only a noise as light as a hedgehog in the grass made him look ahead.

A youth, armed and hooded, stood in his way. Nor did he move as Robin came on, not even that half step to the side that custom allowed for so that two might pass without hindrance.

There was a challenge in his stance. Robin allowed his thoughts to turn to the stranger for a moment. A page, maybe, a squire from the castle, showing his boldness, hoping for an encounter he could boast about afterwards.

If so, Robin was in no mood for such games. He spoke mildly.

57

"Make room, pray, young sir. And I'll make room for you."

The stripling did not move. His eyes in the shadow of his hood were fixed on Robin.

He shrugged and stepped a pace to the right so as to pass. The other stepped, but the same way, blocking the path again. If this was a joke, thought Robin, it was a poor one. If it was a challenge, it was folly.

Robin's voice became stern. "Let me pass, sir!" But still there was no answer, no move aside. Instead, the boy's gloved hand went to his sword hilt.

"Very well." Robin smiled to give the encounter the air of a game. "Have your wish. Look to you."

He threw himself on guard so suddenly that the other stumbled back from the gleaming sword point.

Robin laughed and the sound braced his opponent who drew, turned lightly about and thrust so strongly that the edge of his blade grazed Robin's knuckles. The steel clashed, they drew apart, changed feet and came in once more.

Robin defended himself but did not lunge again. He wished the youth no harm. It would be a sin, he felt, to fight to wound or kill one so young for so little cause.

But the more he parried, the more his challenger pressed him, hacking and cutting, furious at Robin's refusal to fight in earnest.

Now the forest quiet was broken by the ring of steel and the gasp of breath. As Robin drew back, so the stranger came on. Each parry brought a more furious lunge, a wilder cut.

Until Robin stumbled on a root. The other's blade caught his temple and the blood came streaming down his face.

In the sharpness of the pain he cut back so fiercely that the boy flew away and stretched his length on the turf.

Robin stepped forward, sword point at the other's chest.

"Now will you let me pass?" he asked, laughing.

There was no answer. The eyes were closed. The light tunic was slashed across the shoulder and blood soaked scarlet down the side.

The hood had fallen down, the long fair hair spread lightly out across throat and chin. Robin gazed in horror.

"Marian!"

He dropped on one knee, pulling the tunic from the shoulder, ripping the cloth to show the wound deep in the white flesh. Still the eyes were closed. As he bent his ear, he heard the faint flutter of a heartbeat.

"Marian!" He spoke louder as if to wake her. But the eyes stayed closed.

"Robin!"

Men were calling from the track and leaping through the bushes. First was Little John.

"We heard your swords. Why did you not call us?"

Then the tall man stopped and dropped on one knee.

"Maid Marian! Have you killed her?"

"No, but not for want of trying."

The words were spoken faintly. But it was her voice. The eyes were open and on the bloodless face was a smile of triumph.

Friar Tuck bent over them.

"Ah me, the course of love is strange." He beckoned to two outlaws.

"Take up this maid and carry her to our Trysting Tree. I'll go and mix herbs."

He turned his head to Robin.

"She will live and so will you."

So Marian came to Sherwood and made one with the outlaws for a while.

Friar Tuck joined her hands with Robin's, though he said there was no need for they were Green Lord and Lady already. That day there was eating and drinking in plenty, and for the next seven days.

But, when the smoke from the midsummer fires was in the air, Marian went back to her own folk.

"We'll meet again in spring," she promised.

ENTER GUY
OF GISBOURNE

One night Robin's dream returned. He saw two baleful figures, dark brown against the trees. First came Sir Roger, then the yeoman clad in horse hide, mane and tail, the man without a name.

They fell on him, beat him and bound him. Only morning light and waking put an end to his ordeal.

Robin rose from his bracken bed and told Little John of his dream. But when his huge comrade tried to put heart in him, told him to throw this fancy from his mind, Robin was impatient.

"This is no dream. This is a warning. I shall meet these two again, knight and yeoman, together or one by one and I shall be revenged on them. It is my life or theirs."

Little John knew better than to argue. When Robin Hood said, "Go with me, help me find them in the forest," he said nothing, but took his bow and followed his master.

All morning they ranged through the woods, roaming familiar, well-loved tracks, shooting as they went. Little John was cheerful, joking. But Robin was grim and did not smile. Then, towards noon, in the distance, they caught sight of a tall man, leaning on a tree. "That's him, the yeoman from my dream," said Robin, speaking low.

"You stay here, Master," answered Little John. "I'll go and talk to him, find out why he's here and what he seeks."

But these well-meant words were rudely answered. Robin said: "You think nothing of me, Little John, if you believe I'd send another man in front, while I waited in the rear."

He glared at the tall man. "If it were not for bursting my good bow, I'd thrash you for it."

Now Little John was angry in his turn. If that was how Robin Hood would have it, then he'd no more to say. He strode away from Robin, leaving him staring at the waiting man in brown.

Following trails that he knew well, Little John went further north, then east into Barnesdale. Some of the band were hunting there that morning. He'd join them and put quarrel and insult out of his mind.

Two hours pacing and loping along the woodland tracks brought him to the dales. But as he came out into open country, what he saw filled him with anger and alarm. His friends were not hunting now, they were the hunted.

Three outlaws were running for their lives across the glade and into green cover. Two others lay dead on the ground. And after them came the Sheriff's men, a dozen strong and more, and gaining fast.

With a great yell, Little John sprang forward and put himself between pursuers and pursued. Unslinging his bow he took aim, fixing on the man-at-arms whose speed had carried him beyond the others. The arrow flew and down went the Sheriff's man.

But when Little John drew again, opening his shoulders, the bow, young yew wood, splintered in his great hands.

Cursing, he threw away the useless weapon and reached for his sword. Yet before the blade could leave the scabbard, they were on him, seizing arms and legs and leaping upon his back.

He fought like a lion but for once they were too many. In the end, they roped him round and tied him to a tree.

A horseman, fully armed, rode up. Little John knew that harsh and haughty face in the instant. It was the Sheriff of Nottingham himself and he grinned with ferocious pleasure when he saw the prize.

"Ha. Reynold Greenleaf. You have a debt to pay. My plundered kitchen and my strong room. The shame you put me to in Robin Hood's lair. Well, you shall pay that debt, but not now.

"First we shall hunt down your fellows. Then into the cart, and up the hill to swing at the rope's end. This is the day when Robin Hood and his thieving crew will die as they deserve."

Little John looked at him fearlessly. "Maybe that is so and maybe it is not. You are not the one to say when I shall die. If it is my time, so be it. But if not, neither you nor any of your men can kill me."

The Sheriff glowered, then wheeled his horse away.

As Robin came closer down the track, the brown-clad yeoman stood up from the tree and greeted him in friendly manner. Robin did the same. For all his fear and hate, he must know more of this man and what he was after in the forest.

The yeoman looked him over, bow, arrow, sword and dagger. "You're a real archer, I can tell. You must know the greenwood like your home."

"Well enough," answered Robin.

"I've missed my way and am late. Can you set me right?"

Robin nodded. "I'll lead you through the wood. But where are you bound and what's your business?"

"I'm after an outlaw called Robin Hood. I'd rather lay hands on him than have forty pounds in gold."

Robin smiled grimly to himself. This was a bounty hunter. He had been right. And by the look of him he had done more than one good man to death. But to the man he smiled and said, all innocence, "If you met Robin Hood, you'd soon find out who was the better man."

The other laughed. "How about you? How do you stand? Shall we give it a trial?"

"Gladly," answered Robin. He wasted no more time but took his hunting knife and cut a straight wand from a thicket, then bound a bunch of twigs and leaves to the tip. Next he set up the stick, choosing a good long clear space amid the trees.

They disputed for a while about who should shoot first. But then Robin led off, his arrow missing the garland by the merest inch.

The yeoman drew, slow but sure and his shaft landed inside the twig bunch at the head of the wand.

But Robin's next arrow sliced the stem in two and the other raised his hand in respect. "God's name! You're a fine shot. I'd wager you're as good as Robin Hood. Tell me who you are."

Robin shook his head. "First tell me your name."

The other's look was dark and strange.

"I live here and there. I've done things in my time, some I won't talk of. But those who know me call me Guy of Gisbourne."

Robin answered, "I live here in greenwood. And I count you for nothing. I'm the man you're looking for. I am Robin Hood of Barnesdale. As for you, Gisbourne, you're a traitor to men and always have been."

On that dire word, two swords left the scabbard as one, crossed, clashed and flew apart as both men dodged and looked for an opening.

This was a fight to the end. One of them would leave this spot, but only one. They leapt and lunged, swung and struck, the metal flashing in the sun, grating on the sword guards and thudding on the bucklers as they struggled each one to master the other. They fought while the sun moved on from its highest point and the sweat ran down their bodies like rain.

Robin was first to falter, stumbling off guard for the space of a breath. He felt fire in his side as Guy's blade caught him a deadly blow. All strength left his limbs. He sank on one knee and the light fled from his eyes. Seeing nothing, he knew that Gisbourne now raised his sword, two-handed, to bring it down in the last blow. His time had come.

"Dear Lady, Mother mine," the words sounded in his head, "it is no man's fate to die before his time."

He made one last great effort.

The Sheriff swung his horse around and looked down at Little John, face full of triumph.

"Hear that horn, wolf's head? Hear that horn over the dale?"

Little John said not a word. But he heard the horn blow once, twice, thrice, each blast coming closer.

"Good news," said the Sheriff. "That is Guy of Gisbourne. That horn tells me he has killed Robin Hood. Now I have master and man."

He pointed. "Here he comes."

From the cover of the trees emerged the powerful figure of the yeoman, dressed in his horse-hide cloak, hood with its flowing mane pulled over his head, bow at his back and sword at his side.

In his left hand he bore another bow, a quiver and a sword which he held in the air. The right hand was hidden behind his back.

But as he approached he raised it up. The watchers shuddered.

In the right hand was a severed head, face covered in hair and bloodied wounds.

The Sheriff braced himself. "Welcome, Gisbourne. Now is the time to name your reward. Ask and I shall pay, as I promised."

The answer was short: "Keep your gold, sir, I do not need it. I want only one thing."

"What is that?"

"Now I have killed the master, let me slay the man."

"You're a madman," retorted the Sheriff. "You could have earned enough to buy you a knighthood. Still, have your way. Robin Hood's man stands by the tree, bound hand and foot. Strike home!"

Throwing down the bloodied head, the yeoman advanced. A broad blade knife flashed in the sun. The Sheriff's men pressed close behind, but the man in horse hide waved them back.

"Keep off. No one shall hear a man's confession when he is to die. Keep off."

As they stood back, he stepped close to Little John. The knife blade rose and fell. In three swift strokes John's bonds fell to the ground. He heard a whisper.

"Take Gisbourne's bow, John. Back to the tree and let us fight side by side like friends."

They faced about, arrows strung. But before one shot could be loosed, the Sheriff and his men were flying for their lives amid the trees.

Robin took Little John's hand. "Come, let's away home. We've both been close to death this day. But Our Lady watched over us."

"Aye," agreed Little John. "Our time's not yet come."

THE MONK'S REVENGE

I t was a Sunday morning. Birds sang in the trees. Little John looked up at the leafy curtain above.

"A good day," he said. "And I'm a happy man. To be alive on such a day. There's nobody happier anywhere," he declared. Then broke off his speech when he saw Robin Hood's face.

For it was still and dark. No smile, no joking word. A heavy mood hung over him and had done for many days.

"Cheer up," John urged him. "A fine day, a good heart."

But Robin did not reply. He was listening. A light breeze carried the faint sound of a distant bell. He spoke in a low voice.

"I'll go to church. Our Lady had me in mind. I have forgotten her."

Much heard Robin's words and called out to him, "If you do that, Master, then take a dozen men, well armed, with you. Then no one will dare touch you."

"No," answered Robin. "I must go alone. If anyone comes with me, it shall be Little John, to bear my bow."

The tall man spoke and sharply: "I'll come but carry your own bow and I'll carry mine." Then he laughed. "I'll shoot with you, penny a time, on the way."

"A penny a shot?" said Robin. "I'll wager three pennies to your one."

They took their bows and set off through the woods towards the town, shooting at stick targets as they went. But as they shot, so they fell out again.

"That's five shillings you owe me," claimed John.

"Five shillings? Never." Robin was angry.

John stuck to his word. "Pay up," he demanded.

Robin's mood grew even darker, till in a fury he struck Little John.

Out came the big man's sword.

"No man strikes me! If you were not my master, you'd feel the edge of this."

Then he mastered his rage and thrust back his sword saying calmly, "Get yourself a man somewhere else."

Turning his back on Robin he strode away, leaving Robin to go on his own.

The streets of the town were quiet and the church quieter still as Robin went in. Heads turned, and turned back. Worshippers eyed one another. Soon everyone in church knew who had come. But no word was spoken and no one moved.

Robin Hood knelt down to pray. But as he did another person entered and stood in the aisle, looking about him. It was a monk, a stout figure with a massive head. His turning eye fixed on the kneeling man in green. That face he knew. He remembered it well, too well.

Silently he turned and hurried from the chuch. First he ran to the gates and called to the porter to bar them and let no one out. Then to the castle to speak urgently to the Sheriff.

"That traitor Robin Hood, king's felon, wolf's head, the thief who robbed me of the church's gold," he cried.

"What of him?" demanded the Sheriff.

"He's at mass in the church. Go now, my lord, and you'll have him. If he gets away...."

The Sheriff gave orders and armed himself. Then, at the head of a great troop of soldiers, he marched to the church.

As they stormed through the doors, Robin leapt to his feet, cursing his own foolishness. "If only Little John were here," he told himself. "Why did I quarrel with him?"

He drew his two-edged sword and felled the first attacker with a scything blow. Then, swinging and hacking, he cleared space around him, heading always for the door and the chance of a dash for freedom.

Never had he fought like this, in such a place, against such odds. Men screamed as the steel went home. Bodies fell twisting in agony.

Yet no one could touch Robin as he cut his way towards the bright sunlight in the open doorway.

Now he was face to face with the Sheriff himself. Their swords crossed. Robin's sped upwards, throwing the Sheriff's blade aside. Then he brought his own down two-handed on his adversary's head.

With a grinding clash, the sword broke on the Sheriff's helmet.

"Curse the smith that made you," he swore.

"Take him alive," yelled the Sheriff.

The struggle lasted only a brief moment, then Robin Hood was overpowered and dragged away.

When Little John reached the Trysting Tree in Sherwood, the dire news had gone before him.

Much said, "The High Cellarer of St Mary's, him we took eight hundred pounds from, has had his revenge. Our master's in jail under the castle walls. And the monk has his reward. Tomorrow he'll ride to London with letters for the King to tell him Robin Hood is taken."

Little John looked round at the stricken faces of his comrades. Angrily, he rallied them.

"For the sake of Him that died on the Tree stand up now like men. Shame on you to whine like this. Robin Hood has been in danger many times before, and come clear. Listen to me. He's served Our Lady well and will do so again. Trust in her. She'll not let him die.

"Now, this we shall do. Much and I will go to the high road and lie in wait for that monk. Once I lay hands on him, I'll have his blood. The rest of you stay here. Keep to our Trysting Tree. Hunt the deer. Let all go on as if Robin Hood were with you. We shall return."

"My uncle's house looks out on the road south," Much told him. "If we keep watch there the monk cannot get by unseen."

That night John and Much slept in the house by the highway and come the morning they were ready. From the upstairs window they saw two horses coming down from Nottingham. One carried a huge monk in heavy cowl and robe, the second a servant. The High Cellarer travelled light. His business was urgent.

Little John called from the shadow of the house.

"Sir Monk? Are you from Nottingham way?"

The monk reined in, and spoke with pompous pride.

"I am bound for London. I'll have audience with the King."

"Then God save you, Master," said John. "Tell me, have you news from the city? Folk say that wolf's head, Robin Hood, was taken yesterday and lies in jail. Is that so?"

The monk nodded, and took up the reins again. But Little John spoke again. "Why, God's blessing on you. A fine day's work. He robbed me and my friends of twenty marks."

The monk replied with satisfaction. "Yes, he plundered me of a hundred times that sum and more. But I was the one who laid hands on him yesterday and you can thank me for that."

"Better still, sir monk," Little John's voice was ingratiating, "my friend and I will come down and guard you through the wood. Robin Hood still has desperate men who'd be revenged upon you."

Gladly, the monk reined in his horse once more, as Much and Little John ran down into the road. In the very moment that the monk knew truly who his escort was, Little John's hand was at his throat, tumbling him like a sack of corn from the saddle, full on to his head in the road.

Half-dazed, he saw the great sword gleam and shrieked for mercy.

But the outlaw answered, "Mercy? You'll get the mercy you showed Robin Hood. He was my master. You'll never get to the King to tell what you've done."

Down came the sword. The monk's huge head rolled from his shoulders before another cry could come from it. Just as quietly died his servant, at Much's hand. Their secret vanished with their bodies under the turf of the greenwood.

The King looked down from his seat at the two green-clad yeomen who knelt before him. Open in his hand was the Sheriff's letter.

"So, Robin Hood is taken?"

"God save you, sir, that's so," answered Little John.

"Then welcome, good yeoman." The King raised his hand. "There is no man I am more glad to see than you. But this letter speaks of a monk. What has become of him?"

"Alas, Majesty. He died on the way."

The King spoke to his officers.

"Give these yeomen twenty pounds. They shall be my messengers to the Sheriff."

The city gates were locked as Little John and Much rode up. They called the porter with a thunderous knock.

"Open up. Why is the gate barred at noon?"

"Because Robin Hood's in jail and shall stay there till he hangs," came the answer. "He and his men have killed too many in this town."

"Then open up and tell the Sheriff we have brought the Royal Seal. The news of Robin Hood has filled the King's heart with joy."

"What became of the monk, then, that was to tell the King in London?"

"Why, his majesty was so pleased with him he made him chief Abbot of Westminster."

At this, the gates were opened and the two outlaws admitted to the castle. The Royal Seal was sent into the Sheriff. That night the wine flowed and everyone went to their beds in high humour.

When all was dark, Much and Little John crept to the dungeons and roused the chief jailer.

"Wake up, you rogue. Robin Hood's escaped from prison. You've let him go and you'll pay for it."

Half asleep, the jailer, keys at belt, stumbled from his bed right into the great arms of Little John. Soon the doors were unlocked. Robin Hood was on his feet, a sword thrust into his hand and the three were climbing swiftly down the castle walls. By dawn they were back at the

Trysting Tree in the depths of Sherwood, while Robin's men, amazed, gathered round.

Little John told his master, "So I have done a good deed for a bad. Quit yourself. As for me, I'll be gone, as I told you I would." He began to walk away.

"Never!" said Robin Hood with great force. "You shall be master now, Little John, master over my men and me."

"Never!" Little John turned in his tracks. "No, master I'll never be. Let me be one of your men again, Robin, nothing more, nothing less."

Great cheers rang out. Wine was poured freely. Venison pies and fresh bread were brought out. That day there was celebration in Sherwood. But as the cocks crowed in Nottingham, the Sheriff coming to the jail to take Robin Hood to the gallows, found an empty cell and the jailer lying dead outside it.

First he was dumbfounded, then afraid.

"What shall I do? I never dare face the King and tell him I let Robin Hood go. He will hang me for it."

He ordered the city to be searched, every street and narrow alley. But all in vain. Robin Hood had gone and there was no bringing him back.

In time came the dread summons to London. The Sheriff rode to court and fell on his knees before his sovereign.

But he was told to stand. He did so, but could hardly master his trembling. Still, the King spoke mildly.

"You were tricked by Little John, Sheriff. But so was I. I see that." The voice was sharper. "Otherwise, I would have had you hanged.

"There cannot be three yeomen in the land to match Little John. He was true to his master. He loves Robin Hood better than he loves me. If only men were so loyal to their king."

For a moment the King was silent, then he said, "But Robin Hood shall not mock us. He shall be taken."

"How, my liege?" The Sheriff was in despair. "Twice I thought I had my hands on him yet he escaped."

"Then try once more," declared the King. "Use guile, as Little John did. And, this third time, do not let him go."

A GOLDEN ARROW

ow the word went out from Nottingham Castle that on a certain day a great archery contest would be held. Large butts were set up on the great meadow outside the walls of the city.

All the finest archers in the north country were invited to take part. And for the best archer of all, a fine prize was offered.

It was an arrow, but no common arrow. It had a silver white shaft, a head and feathers of rich red gold. Nothing like it had been seen before.

The Sheriff of Nottingham sent word throughout the north, then waited for the day to see who would claim the golden arrow. For he had in mind an even greater prize.

Under the Trysting Tree in Sherwood, Robin Hood called his company together. They crowded into the glade from all sides, from near and far, seven score strong lads in Lincoln green, bows bent and arrows feathered.

He looked them all over as if to see if all his men were true to him.

"Who'll go with me to the shooting in Nottingham?" he asked.

And as one, they lifted their bows above their heads.

Robin was well pleased. But he said with care, "No more than six of us will join the contest. With me will be Little John, Gilbert White Hand, Will Scarlet, Much the Miller's son and George-a-Green. We shall shoot for the golden arrow and we shall bring it home to Sherwood.

"But all the rest shall go with us and be at hand amid the crowds. Stand by, eyes keen and bows at the ready. For I smell treachery in the air."

So the day came and the green below the City Walls was bright with pennants and flags, the shine of armour and the colour of the crowds, green and blue and scarlet.

Under a large striped awning that lifted in the breeze, stood the Sheriff of Nottingham. In front of him, on a table where all could see, glittered the golden arrow.

He was content. His plans were laid. They could not fail. For Robin Hood could not refuse the challenge. He dared not refuse it. If he failed to appear at the butts today, all the folk in the north country would know he was afraid. Yes, Robin Hood would come and the Sheriff would be waiting for him.

The trumpets called and twenty archers took their turn at the butts. The rivalry was keen, the shooting true and the crowds were on edge.

Within an hour it was clear to all that there were only six archers, tall men in green and red, who were in contention. One of these six would claim the golden prize.

One by one they shot. The huge figure of Little John led the way, then bold Will Scarlet and Much the Miller's son. Robin himself shot fourth, then Gilbert White Hand and George-a-Green, the Wakefield champion.

Three times they shot to decide the issue. And three times Robin Hood's arrow split the mark exactly in two. A great shout rose from the crowded meadow. Such shooting had not been seen in years.

And now the keen-eyed man in red and green advanced to the space before the Sheriff's awning. The crowd grew silent as if they knew the game had ended, but another game, more deadly, had begun.

Robin moved forward steadily, back straight, face calm but alert, bow in his left hand. As he reached the prize stand, he threw back his hood, bowed to the Sheriff, his ladies and his officers. The Sheriff rose, but instead of stepping to the table where the golden arrow shone in the afternoon sunlight, he raised a mail-gloved hand.

Horns blew. From all around, men-at-arms, swords drawn, rushed to form a great circle, hemming in crowd and contestants and all. The ambush was laid, the trap was sprung.

Robin calmly stepped to the table, took the arrow and held it up for all to see, then facing the Sheriff spoke in a voice that carried over the hushed throng.

"Woe to you, Sheriff. Your way is evil. Had you come to Sherwood for a match, I would have given you safe conduct."

"Wolf's head!" snarled the Sheriff, sharp and pale with hatred. And at his words, six soldiers rushed from behind the tent and closed on Robin.

In that instant, Robin gave a signal and turning threw himself down. Like a rush of wind, arrows flew from the heart of the crowd. Down went the men-at-arms. Another volley poured among the Sheriff's officers. Screams filled the air, confusion, men and women ran or rolled upon the ground.

The crowd scattered and in their midst was seen a great company of men in green, massed in ranks, back to back, half facing the Sheriff's tent, half facing the surrounding soldiers.

Robin at their head, and Little John by his side, they trotted forward, shooting as they moved. The circling band of men-at-arms broke and ran, leaving a way clear from the meadow.

"After them, cut them off," the Sheriff's voice was heard.

"Forward," answered Robin and the outlaws ran towards the distant green of the woods. On either side, the ambushing troops fell back, some out of fear, some with arrows in their hearts.

But one was down on Robin's side. An arrow from the flank struck home in Little John's knee. The great man rolled, teeth clenched, upon the grass.

"Forward," commanded Robin once more. The outlaws ran towards the trees. Robin and Much heaved Little John to his feet, only to see him drop again.

"Master," he groaned. "Now leave me here. But not alive. As you love me, for all the years I've served you, take out your sword and cut off my head. Don't let them take me."

"Never," said Robin, "not for all the gold in England."

"God forbid," Much told his wounded comrade. "By Him that died on the Tree, you'll not leave our band like that."

They raised him on their shoulders and ran after the others. Behind them came the Sheriff's men, some mounted, pressing closer.

At every fifty yards they laid John down and turned to shoot, sending the men-at-arms spinning from their horses. Then they took him up and struggled on.

Soon they would reach the shelter of the forest. But their pursuers came up so fast, Robin began to see they would not get clean away.

"We must stand and fight here," he called, "or we shall never reach our Trysting Tree."

"No, no," Little John gasped in his pain. "There is another chance, Robin. Just within the forest, to the west, lies Sir Richard's castle. If we can reach him, we've a chance of safety."

Sir Richard's men came running to call him to the castle walls. He hastened to look out over the forest.

Through the trees he saw the outlaw band in full retreat, turning now and then to loose off a cloud of arrows, then hurrying on again.

Now he could see the hunters, scores of them, armed and mounted, drawing closer.

Swiftly, Sir Richard went into the courtyard, shouting to his servants, "Open the gates, let down the bridge."

Then to his men-at-arms: "Take station on the walls."

The gates swung back, the bridge rumbled down on its chains and over the way to safety pounded the outlaw band, breath bursting in their chests.

As Robin and Much, bearing Little John between them, staggered into the courtyard, the knight commanded, "Draw the bridge. Shut the gates."

The bridge clanked up, the gates crashed home. Outside, the Sheriff and his men reined in their horses, massing below the walls, glaring up in helpless fury.

Inside, Sir Richard greeted Robin.

"Welcome, Robin. Welcome to you and all your men. Now is the time to repay the kindness done to me, by the man I love more than any in this world."

He gave orders for Little John to be cared for and food and wine to be brought for Robin's men.

Then, with his sword drawn, he climbed once more to his castle walls and looked down on the Sheriff's troop.

"Traitor!" the Sheriff's voice was hoarse with anger. "Those are the King's enemies. Help them and you place yourself outside the law."

Looking down, the knight answered calmly.

"Sir, I have done nothing I will not stand by. Go home with your men. There is nothing you can do here. I shall surrender this castle and these men only to the King himself and not to you."

Silent, the Sheriff turned about. The castle, double-ditched and walled and well defended, could defy any force he had.

From Sir Richard's walls the outlaws watched in triumph as their enemies retreated, heading back for Nottingham.

The knight told Robin Hood: "When all your men are well and rested you may go back to greenwood. Nottingham will not dare attack unless the King gives leave."

Robin thanked him. "Good knight, you've saved our lives today and we will not forget. For I will wager all I have that today is not the end of this. We shall beware, both you and me. More treachery is on the way."

In London the King heard all that the Sheriff had to tell him.

"Is what you tell me true? Sir Richard is a noble knight."

"Sire, to my face, the knight avowed everything he had done to help your enemy Robin Hood. But there is more to this, my liege. Sir Richard has his plans. He will be lord of all the North and defy your rule."

The King rose. His face was hard.

"I will deal with this. In a fortnight's time I'll be in Nottingham. I will take Robin Hood and the knight myself. Now, go home, Sheriff. Do as I tell you. Gather up all the men you can, archers above all. Then wait until I come."

Riding home to Nottingham, the Sheriff brooded on the King's words. He had other plans and they would not wait until the King rode north.

SIR RICHARD MUST DIE!

"A rider," warned the look-out. "Horse on the forest road!"

Robin waited with his men under the Trysting Tree as the sound of hooves drew closer. There was no danger, only mystery. Who could be coming this way, so early, so urgently?

"Make way," commanded Robin as he saw through the trees at the far end of the glade, a palfrey, richly harnessed but hard-ridden and stumbling. On its back was a woman in grey, bent over the saddle.

As the beast dragged to a halt, Robin strode forward and took the bridle, while Little John carefully helped the rider dismount. Then Robin and Little John threw back their hoods and knelt on the grass.

"My lady!"

It was Sir Richard's wife, her face pale with alarm.

"Help me, sir!" Her voice was still breathless. "Help me for our Dear Lady's sake."

Robin rose and led her to the bank beneath the Tree where both sat down. He sent for wine, but she would not drink and only said again, "Help me, sir."

"What has happened?" Robin asked. But even before she answered he knew why she had come.

"Don't let them kill my lord, Sir Richard!"

Robin leapt up. "Who'd dare to threaten your lord with death?"

She answered wearily: "At dawn, he rode by the river, hunting with his hawks. A squire was with him, when the Sheriff of Nottingham's men seized and bound him hand and foot. The squire escaped to bring the news to me. They have taken him to Nottingham Castle. I fear they'll kill him before the sun sets today."

Robin swore: "By the Rood! Only the King can take Sir Richard. And the King is still in London."

"True, and the Sheriff means to strike first."

"I smell a rat." Little John, standing by, put in a word. "The Sheriff means to use Sir Richard as bait to lure you out of the forest, Master. He knows you'll never let the knight die."

"True," answered Robin, "yet if I hide here, Sir Richard may die, and shamefully."

He raised his voice so that all in the glade heard him and came running.

"Bows and swords! Bows and swords!"

Will Scarlet added his warning: "Nottingham will be full of soldiers. The Sheriff's scoured the country for men-at-arms."

"We'll find a way," said Robin. "Little John shall lead our company to the green before the city walls. Lie round about, but all stay hidden."

To Sir Richard's wife, he said, "My lady, be pleased to stay here. You will be safe. Before the sun's at noon, we'll bring Sir Richard to you. Or we shall not return ourselves."

When the men in Lincoln green had surrounded the meadow, Robin made ready to enter the city on his own. He told Little John.

"This must be done by stealth. They'll bring the knight out to the green and wait for us to strike. But if we do they'll kill him before we can get near. Someone must be close to him, then, and that's a task for me alone."

"Master, what will you do?"

"Trust to Our Lady. Somewhere on the road, I'll find the means."

He set off boldly to the gates. Now the sun was well up, the daily coming and going had begun, carts and folk with bundles on their backs passing to and fro.

And like a miracle, among the crowds, he spotted what he sought. An old man, a pilgrim beggar, one whose days had once been good, but now were good no longer.

His great cloak was patched with black, blue and red squares, his breeches, too. His hose were darned from knee to foot and his shoes mended top and bottom. About his neck and shoulders were bags for food and odds and ends. He was a sorry sight.

But he still had his pride. When Robin greeted him, "Hey, old man. What will you take to change clothes with me?" he answered, "Why make mock of an old man?"

"No, gaffer," Robin told him, "don't be cross. I mean what I say. I'll give you forty shillings for your gear. I've a fancy to wear it and have a jest with the Sheriff."

He pulled the coins from his pouch. The old man looked at the money, at Robin, then made up his mind. They turned aside into an alley and the exchange was made in a trice. The ancient went on his way, happy in his new green tunic, while Robin sniffing at his outfit, marched into the city.

He did not have far to walk. For there in the main street, in the midst of a great crowd, with his men-at-arms, rode the Sheriff. Behind them in a cart, erect and in his shirtsleeves, head bare, hands tied behind him, stood Sir Richard of the Lee.

Crowing and capering, Robin threw himself into the way, right under the hooves of the Sheriff's horse, making it rear and bringing the cavalcade to a halt.

"My lord, a boon, my lord!" he cried in a high cracked voice.

The Sheriff pulled on his bridle and looked down.

"What boon, old fool?"

"I'll wager, my lord, you have no one to be your executioner this day."

The Sheriff did not say a word. For it was true. There wasn't a man in Nottingham would dare lay hands on Sir Richard, his name was so good, his reputation so high. This was a game of bluff the Sheriff played and the old man's words came close to the bone.

"What will you give an old man who'll do the work?" piped Robin.

The Sheriff laughed but had to answer. Under the filthy hood, the old man's gleaming eye transfixed him.

"The hangman's wage, thirteen pence and three new suits. And those you need, old man. But this is heavy work. Are you equal to it?" the Sheriff mocked.

To his astonishment, the old fool began to leap up and down, turning somersaults under the horse's noses and making the beasts rear up again.

"Done, old man," the Sheriff laughed, "the job is yours. Now make way and let us get to the green."

The oldster pranced to one side. The execution party pressed forward to the gate. But now the beggar leapt nimbly into the cart and the guard, who stood beside Sir Richard, turned up his nose as the smell from the rags reached him.

As the horses clattered through the gate and out into the great green space below the walls, Sir Richard heard the old man speak in his ear.

"Be of good cheer, noble knight. This is the best day of your life."

The guard laughed coarsely. "Shut your mouth, you old devil."

But the beggar went on. "Believe me, sir knight, I've lived a long time. Man's life is misery. Yours will soon end."

With a great effort, the knight kept still and pretended he had not heard. The cart rolled on and came to rest on the green.

Around in a great square stood ranks of men-at-arms. A little further off, the great crowd waited silently. The sun now shone above the trees but the breeze was cold. Sir Richard shivered.

"What, afraid, sir knight?" the Sheriff called.

Sir Richard answered coldly.

"Not I, of you, Nottingham. Give me a sword and I will fight you and your men, one by one or altogether. I'll not die like a dog."

"You will, false knight," the Sheriff jeered. "Friend

and protector of thieves." The Sheriff looked around him. "But where is the man you befriended now?"

"He's here, you dog!"

A great roar came from the cart. Sheriff and men were still, robbed of speech or breath, as the old man made four swift movements, almost in the same instant. He threw off his patched cloak, cut Sir Richard's bonds, snatched the sword out of the guard's scabbard and handed it to the knight, then leapt from the cart.

Now the two stood back to back, blade in hand, in the cool morning. Recovered from their shock, the Sheriff's men rushed forward.

But even as they ran, they shrieked and choked and fell, arrows in throat, in chest, in back and side, and from the bushes round about came the green rout of Robin's men. For a moment, Nottingham and his officers stood their ground. But their men were in full flight back to the city where the fearful crowd already blocked the gates.

Wheeling, the Sheriff fled for his life. But before his horse had gone ten yards, Little John took aim. The yard-long shaft struck through from back to chest. Fixed through the heart, the Sheriff fell to ground. His horse, stirrups swinging, saddle empty, raced away.

Robin stood over the writhing body, sword raised.

"An evil end to evil. Oath-breaker! While you lived, no man could trust you. Now you die, no man shall mourn you."

Up went the great blade, glinted a moment in the sun, then fell like a stone. The body shook, the head leapt away from it. Nottingham's Sheriff was gone. Robin bowed to the knight.

"Sir, you must learn now to run and leave your steed behind. Come to greenwood where your lady has gone before you. Stay with us until the King rides north. Then we shall both await his grace."

A King
Disguised

The King rode north from London with knights and armed men at his back. For he was angry. His officer, the High Sheriff of Nottingham, beheaded, and his corpse left outside the city gates like a traitor or felon.

And the once loyal knight, Sir Richard of the Lee, fled with his lady into Sherwood, taking refuge with Robin Hood and his outlaw band.

Riding into Nottingham, the King proclaimed that whoever could place Robin Hood into his hands would earn a rich reward.

He sent his men throughout the north country, commanding them to seek out Robin Hood and Sir Richard and bring them to justice.

For six months they scoured the land, but returned empty-handed. They found the secret places in the forest, but no one was there. The outlaws and their guests had vanished like rain into grass, leaving no trace.

What was even more bitter, each search party brought news of how the deer stock in the Royal forests had diminished. While the King's officers hunted outlaws in one part of the woods, the outlaws hunted the King's venison in another.

Day by day, as more bad tidings reached him, the King's fury grew. He let it be known that the castle and lands of Sir Richard of the Lee were forfeit. Anyone who captured or killed the knight would have all he owned and keep it for his family, one generation after another.

But when this was proclaimed, an old knight, long in the King's service, asked leave to speak to him.

"My liege lord, if you love any man, do not give them what belongs to Sir Richard."

The King frowned. "Why do you say that?"

"Sire, no man who takes Sir Richard's castle will hold it while Robin Hood's alive and carries bow or sword."

Angry though he was, the King knew that these words were wise. "What shall I do?" he asked.

Bowing, the old knight answered: "There is a man who can help you, Majesty."

"Bring him to me."

They brought a grey-bearded forester whose long life had passed in Sherwood. He knew each woodland way and track.

"My lord!" he dropped on one knee. "I can take you so close to Robin Hood, you may talk with him and lay hands on him, if you wish."

"How?" the King demanded.

And the forester told the King what he must do.

One May morning, when the forest was still, no sign of King's men throughout its length and breadth, Robin Hood's men took their ease beneath the Trysting Tree.

Word came from a lookout that travellers were on the high road. Sir Richard told his lady wife: "Now you will see how Robin Hood treats wayfarers who come into his greenwood."

In a little while a party of six grey-clad monks appeared on horseback, followed by laden packhorses. In front rode an abbot, a great figure, head shrouded in a vast cowl.

Robin Hood stepped out and took the Abbot's bridle.

"Sir Abbot," he said courteously, "stay with us for a while. We are all yeomen here who live by hunting the King's deer and by the charity of travellers like you. Sir, you and your churches have land and gold. What can you offer us?"

Speaking in a muffled voice, the Abbot answered: "There is no more than forty pounds in my bag. I've been in Nottingham with the King for a fortnight. Most of my gold has gone in feasting lords and ladies."

He handed over his money bag and watched Little John count out the money. "The Abbot is true," the big man said. Robin divided the money into two parts, one to his men, the other he handed back to the Abbot. "You will need this for your spending," he said.

"Thank you," the Abbot told him, then from his sleeve he took out something which, as he held it up, caused Robin Hood to fall on one knee.

"The King's seal!"

"Yes, and my lord the King bids you come to Nottingham."

Robin rose: "We are all loyal to the King. We bid you welcome with his seal. You must dine with us today."

He led the Abbot and his monks to the space below the great tree, where cloths were laid with venison, white bread, red wine and beer. Bowls of water were there for washing.

The Abbot stared curiously as a plump friar said grace and then with a wink, raised his cup and invited the guests to fall to and eat.

When the meal was done, Robin Hood turned to the Abbot. "Now, sir, you shall see how we live, and tell the King of it."

Lifting the horn from his belt, he blew three blasts and from the trees around scores of men in green bounded in, armed with bow and sword. Standing in ranks, they saluted Robin Hood with a great shout that made the Abbot flinch.

Archery wands were set up, each one topped with a rose garland. Then shooting began at fifty paces, after Robin Hood declared, "Any man who misses the garland even by three fingers' breadth, forfeits his tackle, and what's more gets a buffet over the ear. No one will be spared."

Nor were they. Everyone who missed the mark got a swinging blow from Robin that rocked him on his heels.

Then Robin took his turn and twice he split the wand. But on the third shot he was out of luck, the arrow flew by, and Gilbert White Hand called out jokingly, "Now for you, Master, to get your pay. Stand forth and take it like a man."

Robin laughed and offered his bow and quiver to the chief guest.

"Sir Abbot, I surrender my gear to you. Now," he threw back his hood, "serve me as I served my men."

The Abbot was unwilling. "I would not strike a yeoman for fear of doing injury."

But Robin only laughed even more. "Strike, sir, I give you all the leave you need."

Standing, the Abbot bared his arm, and Little John, standing near, opened his eyes wider, as he saw the knotted muscles under the sleeve. Strange man of the church, thought he.

Now the arm swung up and struck home. Robin was knocked head over heels and his men let out a great shout. Leaping to his feet, Robin took hold of the Abbot's arm.

"There's strength in you, sir monk."

Then he stared hard. For the Abbot's cowl had fallen onto his shoulders showing a handsome, sunburnt face and fair, curled hair. Sir Richard and his lady, standing close by, dropped to their knees. Then Robin followed their example and all the men in the glade.

"My lord," said Robin, "now I know you. Mercy for me and all my men, as God may save us. Mercy, I beg you."

The King looked down at Robin.

"Pardon is granted, Robin Hood, to you and all your men, but there is one condition. This outlaw life must cease. You must all leave Sherwood and, so that I know that you are true, you shall come to court and serve me there."

For a moment, Robin said nothing, then, "I vow to God it shall be so. I'll come to court and all my company shall be your men."

"Rise, Robin Hood," the King commanded. Looking round at the outlaw band, he asked, "Will you sell me green cloth for me and my knights."

"Gladly," Robin answered. "What we have is yours, for another day you may clothe me."

So the "monks" threw off their grey habits and put on Lincoln green, King as well. All set out for Nottingham, playing at shoot and strike as they went. Robin Hood and the King swapped blows in sport.

"This is a game to learn," laughed the King. "Though if I tried for a year, I'd not get the better of you with bow and arrow."

When the citizens of Nottingham, the Sheriff's men among them, looked out from the walls, they saw a green-clad army riding and marching towards them across the meadows.

"Robin Hood's come to town," the fearful cry went up. "He'll kill us all." And officers, servants, even old women on sticks, began to fly for their lives as the forest horde entered the city.

But the King stood up from the saddle and told them: "Come back. Don't be afraid." And slowly the runaways crept back and recognized their ruler.

Soon enough fright gave way to joy. Tables were spread. There was feasting and drinking, dancing and singing. The news that Robin Hood and the knight were pardoned spread around.

The King now addressed Sir Richard. "You shall have your land again, sir. Promise me that you will deserve this pardon."

The knight dropped on his knee. "I promise, Majesty."

Robin knelt, too, and the King looked keenly at him.

"Robin Hood, outlaw no longer, but yeoman of the King."

ROBIN ALONE

So Robin Hood and his men left the outlaw life behind and followed the King to London. No more the bracken bed under the stars, the greenwood life, the hunting of the deer, skirmishing with foresters, living free – in peril of death at the end of a rope.

Now the bustle of the King's hall, the heat and clamour of the tourney field, and shooting green, the waiting in place, the following of rule and command.

Their fame went before them. Lords and ladies, knights and squires, soldiers and servants flocked to see them. Their skill with bow and sword was the envy of the world.

Robin was admired on all sides, pointed out, sought after, marvelled at. This was the man who had ruled his robber kingdom, made his own laws, punished Sheriffs, plundered abbots, defied even the King.

Now here he was, standing at his sovereign's knee, listened to and loved, out of the forest and into the palace.

The Queen and her ladies were gracious to him. His courtesy, his goodness to womankind, his generosity to the poor, were the talk of the land.

But what all admired, courtier and yeoman, knight and squire, was Robin's open hand. He had a way that none could match, a warm heart. Where he was, wine and money flowed, all came and none were refused. His was the rule of the greenwood, living for the day, giving and sharing, for tomorrow down the road would come another baron or another bishop, whose saddlebags would pour out fresh gold.

But now only Robin's gold poured out, to pay for his men's food and clothing, to pay for his guests' pleasure. The months went by, the courtly round went on, and so the wealth he brought to court melted away, and one by one, when he could no longer support them, so did his men.

"Go north, lads," he told them. "I've no more to give you. Go back where you belong. No one can touch you. You've the King's pardon. Go home."

"What about you, Master?" they asked.

"I'm bound. I stay here," he answered.

Robin watched them take the road, back to the fields and woods, and with each day and each man going, he grew more silent. Before a year was out, no more of Robin's men remained at court save Little John and Will Scarlet. They longed to go but would not leave him.

The pleasures of the hall soon pale, those of the greenwood last a lifetime. They said no word to him but he knew what was in their thoughts. So when the New Year came he sent them home too and sat alone in London.

One day the Queen beckoned him to her, asking, "Robin, what ails you? Are you sick? There's a dark look on your face we are not used to see."

Robin answered truthfully. "Alas, my lady, once I was the best archer in England, now what am I here? I long to be in Barnesdale or in Sherwood. These past seven nights, I've neither slept nor eaten. If I stay here, I'll die."

The Queen then told him, kindly: "Go and ask the King to let you go, just for a little while. Ask."

Robin knelt before the King.

"Grant me an asking, lord," he said.

"Ask, Robin."

"In Barnesdale Forest, Sire, I have a little place I use as chapel for my Lady Mary. I want to journey there."

The King said: "Granted, for a space. Seven days to go, seven days to stay and seven to make your way back here. But do not forget, you are my man."

Robin promised and made ready for the journey. Next day he left the

noise of the court, the smell and smoke of the city, and marched into the fresh air of the country and the long highway. At first he went swiftly, sang as he walked, and always headed for the north.

But day by day, more doubts came into his mind. How could he live in Barnesdale, all alone? How could he live and not go hunting for the deer? How could he live if no one came when he called to them? The cord-bound horn hung useless at his belt. Harder still, how could he march back south again, leaving the greenwood for the palace?

Brooding, he turned aside and wandered off. Where he went to, no one surely knows, though there are those who claim they saw him.

There are fishermen who'll tell you he worked with them, calling himself Simon, how ill he worked and how they laughed at him. But when they were beset by pirates, this Simon stood against the mast and with his arrows slew the pirate captain and his crew. And afterwards this Simon took their gold and shared it out among the crew and came ashore and gave it to the poor.

If that was so, then that was Robin Hood.

Others will tell you, beggars, tinkers, shepherds, pedlars, how they challenged Robin Hood, quarrelled with him and beat him too, broke his sword and kicked his ribs and left him spewing by the road.

Well, if they did, that was some other Robin, someone with a borrowed name, lost and wandering, tired and sick.

Some say he grew weary, roamed to Kirklees. He stood upon the ridge and looked down in the glen where the priory sits by a dark stream. There in the thick-walled gatehouse nuns tended the sick wayfarer. Robin looked down and thought he'd be bled and tended till his strength returned. The Lady Prioress was kin to him, or so they say. She'd see to him.

But yet again he turned his back and wandered east and south, until his feet led him to Barnesdale. And at last, in mid-winter, he found his secret place amid the leafless trees. His limbs were weak and heavy. So long had passed since he had eaten that hunger no longer touched him, neither in thought nor feeling.

Under the shelter he lay down. His power had almost ebbed away. The cold grew sharper, pierced him through and held him to the ground.

He dreamed that all was well again. He leaned his back on the Trysting Tree and all around were men in green like leaves in summer.

Then that dream faded and another came. Out of the darkness swelled an evil light. And in its middle stood a knight in dark array, all armed and with the cold eye of a priest.

"Die, Robin Hood, for all your wickedness, your time has come."

"Not yet," said Robin, "not till my Lady calls."

Weak as he was, he swung his sword. But the glow vanished and the dark Sir Roger fled away. A cold grey mist was round him.

Sheathing his sword, he knelt and prayed.

"My Lady, speak. Is my time here?"

The grey mist swirled away, the woods around were green. Before him stood a woman dressed in white and green.

"My Lady!" Robin said, and she replied.

"Robin, it's Marian. Come, get up. It's spring again."

She took his hand.

"Robin, come blow your horn."

He blew three blasts and out of the thickets, one by one, they came. Little John, Will Scarlet, Much the Miller's son, George-a-Green, Allan-a-Dale, Friar Tuck and all the rest.

"Welcome to greenwood, Master!"

Then he knew that he could not return to serve the King.

ROBIN BETRAYED

By the rising and setting of the sun, the white of may and the fall of red and yellow leaves, years passed in the forest.

The King's men ceased to hunt for Robin Hood, though his leaving the court was neither forgotten nor forgiven. Nottingham's new Sheriff valued his own head too highly to enter the outlaw strongholds. He kept to his own affairs and left them to theirs.

And men grew older. Robin's band grew smaller. Archers left the woods and went back to the plough and the village. With time, only a score or so were left, men like Little John, Much, Will Scarlet, George-a-Green. They loved the free life in Barnesdale too much to leave it, though each winter the wind blew a little colder, limbs were a little stiffer. They sat or lay in the lodges by the Trysting Tree and talked of old times, adventures and dangers now safely past, never to be again.

A day came at last when Robin felt his strength fail him. His arrows flew weakly, a weariness came over him. He called his nearest men and told them, "I'm not well. There's nothing for it but to have my blood let. I'll go to Kirklees Priory, where my aunt's daughter is the Lady Prioress. They will bleed me and maybe my health and strength will be restored."

Will Scarlet, ever cautious, warned him, "Take a company to guard you, Robin."

Robin was scornful. "Stay at home if you're afraid."

Will replied: "If you are angry, you'll hear no more from me."

Robin shook his head. "No one shall come with me, but Little John may bear my bow."

Little John's voice was heavy. "Bear your own bow. Come, let's shoot a penny as we go."

So there was no quarrel in the end, though a sadness as Robin and John set off westwards for Kirklees.

The sky was grey, the sun hid itself and the woods were sombre as they marched mile after mile, with little to say. At last, near Kirklees, they entered a gloomy vale, where no breeze blew and no birds sang.

"Here's an ill place, Master," said Little John, but Robin strode on.

In the depths of the glen they came on a deep, dark stream. There on a plank sat an old woman, shadowy as the water, muttering curses to herself.

"Who are you cursing, Dame?" asked Robin.

She raised her grey locks and answered, "I curse Robin Hood, who owned no master and no law, who lived by the bow and the sword, dealing out death to many a mother's son, taking what was not his to have. Curse you, Robin Hood, today your blood shall flow."

"Master, let's turn," urged Little John. "There's still a chance to save your life. Don't cross the stream."

Robin set foot on the plank and said, "Little John, when first we met you hindered me from going over water. Do not do it now. Come with me or turn back. Be of good cheer; I shall not die before my day."

Over they went and deeper ran the water, deeper was the shade. Till at a bend, they met three women washing clothes. As they washed, they sang a dirge.

"Who are you mourning, Dames?" asked Robin.

They answered, "We sigh for Robin Hood, whose blood shall flow today. For who will shield the poor and womankind? Who will rebuke the mighty and the false, who will put wrong to right? Who will be King when May returns?"

Little John spoke up again: "Turn back, Robin, while there's time."

"Too late to turn, for Kirklees is below us."

Now the glen ran deeper and hard by the black water lay the Priory. Upon a bridge the gatehouse stood, stout as a keep, with thick walls and narrow windows.

Little John said, "Master, are two warnings not enough for you? I beg you, do not enter."

Robin replied, "Wait there, good John, until I call. The Prioress is my cousin. She would not harm me for the world."

He knocked. A nun took Robin in and John was left outside. The door slammed shut. They led him to an upstairs chamber. Its window looked upon the wooded hill, the clouded sky. Inside, the room was lit by candle flame. A figure at the window turned. The Prioress, handsome and pale, dark-robed with silk at wrist and neck, and silk in her hands, masking the bowl she carried.

"Lie down, cousin Robin. See, here's the chafing dish, the irons, ready to let your blood and draw out all the ill."

Robin took out his purse. "Cousin, here's twenty pounds to pay for all to make me well. And there is more if you have need."

"More than enough," she said. "Lie down and bare your arm."

Gently and skilfully, she slid the cloth along the arm, laid bare the muscles and tied the cord until the blue veins swelled.

"Lie easy, Robin. I'll lance the vein and leave you while the bad blood runs."

The knife cut home, the burden of the blood began to leave him. His head grew light, and visions formed before his eyes, green men and running deer, leaves, laughter, singing.

Now he heard voices outside the open door, whispering his name. The Prioress spoke, then a man. But why should a man be here? Something was wrong. Robin rose on his elbows, striving to see. The candle shone on chafing dish, the red-stained irons, the blood that flowed thin and clear, the stream of life itself.

And as he saw that he groaned, for he knew he had been betrayed. He struggled from the bed as the door swung fully open. There stood the Prioress, a sly smile on her face. But she did not smile at Robin. Her eyes were on the man at her side, as a woman looks at her lover. And that man, dressed in autumn colour, drawn sword glinting in the flame was – Sir Roger, the Red Knight and priest of evil name. This was no fever-vision. His enemy was here in the flesh, winter to kill his spring. Robin drew his sword, but in that instant felt the knight's blade drive into his side.

Not yet! He swung his sword with all his might. The keen edge struck the dark assassin between shoulder and head. Now his blood spurted. Down he went and stretched out on the floor.

"Lie like a dog," said Robin and turned to the window. His strength was failing. But tugging his horn, he gave a final call. Feebly he blew and weakly sank back on the bed, lying with his enemy at his feet. They were alone. The Prioress had fled.

A great hammering on the door below, huge blows breaking the locks, footsteps beating on the stairs. Now Little John's strong arms raised him up.

"They tricked you, Master, as I warned. But there's still time. Let me carry you from this cursed place. And when you're safe, I'll burn the house and all inside."

"No, Little John, you may not," Robin told him. "In all my life I never did woman harm and shall not when I die."

"Die, Master? You're not done yet. Come."

But Robin said: "It's done. My time has come. Give me my bow. Notch me an arrow. Where it falls, so bury me in grass and gravel. Put my sharp sword at my feet, my quiver too, my yew bow by my side, my measuring wand...

"Bury me there so folk will say, 'Here lies bold Robin Hood'."

So his eyes closed.

Upon a ridge above Kirklees is a place where they say Robin Hood is buried. In time the grave was opened. No one and nothing was inside.

Christ have mercy on his soul
That died on the Rood
For he was a good outlaw
And did poor men much good.

AUTHOR'S NOTE

There may have been an outlaw called Robin Hood, in the 12th or 13th century. But he is a shadowy figure, despite much detective work by professional and amateur historians.

Yet Robin Hood, the legend, is excitingly vivid, his picture full of detail, added to, altered, polished by many hands unknown and well known.

As successive ages re-shaped the "Prince of Thieves" in their own image, he has been moved further and further away from his yeoman origins, becoming an Earl who had lost his lands, a supporter of Richard the Lionheart against Prince John, or even a rebel Saxon.

Yet the earliest "tellings", those closest to the legend's origins, speak of neither King Richard nor King John. Instead they speak of King Edward. Richard and John were added centuries later (around 1600) by Elizabethan and Jacobean poets and playwrights, who also turned Robin into an earl. Their only authority was a single date given by a Scots historian, John Major, in 1521. One ballad does feature Richard, but Joseph Ritson the eighteenth-century collector, describes this as hack work by "some miserable retainer of the Press".

I have solved this problem by making the king symbolic (like Robin Hood) and timeless, without a name.

In this re-telling I have tried to get back to the original yeoman outlaw Robin Hood, as his story was first told and sung some six or seven centuries ago.

To do this I have chosen six of the oldest "tellings" and ballads, including the most famous, *A Gest of Robyn Hode*, which is nearly 14,000 words long and contains four adventures. To these I have added all or part of eight ballads of later date. I have chosen only those that offer original stories and are consistent in feeling and meaning with the earliest accounts.

This has involved certain small liberties. To fill out the slender ballad of Maid Marian and the fragments of plays from the time when fifteenth- and sixteenth-century villagers changed their May King and Queen into Robin and Marian, I have drawn on contemporary reports and on the haunting ballad, "The Nut Brown Maid".

In foreshadowing and re-telling the Death of Robin Hood, I have tried to give substance to the shadowy figure of the Red Knight, Sir Roger, as a kind of symbol of autumn-winter, to match Robin's summer-spring. Rather more recklessly I have tried to fill the gap in the "Death" left by damage to the original manuscript.

These slight additions apart, I have held to my intention to retell those stories first told some seven centuries ago, when villains were often in power and honest men sometimes on the run.

England's folk hero needs no "updating", no fabricated noble pedigree, nor motivation for being an outlaw. The message of Robin Hood and his Meinee, that truth, justice and courtesy should be defended, if need be *against* the law, is as valid for the present as for the past.

ROBERT LEESON